AN OCCUPATION
OF ANGELS

ALSO BY LAVIE TIDHAR

NOVELS
*The Tel Aviv Dossier**
*Osama**
The Violent Century
*A Man Lies Dreaming**
Unholy Land
By Force Alone
The Candy Mafia
*Martian Sands**

THE BOOKMAN HISTORIES
The Bookman
Camera Obscura
The Great Game
(also available in omnibus form as *The Bookman Histories*)

NOVELLAS
*New Atlantis**
*The Vanishing Kind**
*Cloud Permutations**
*Jesus & the Eightfold Path**
*Gorel & the Pot-Bellied God**
*The Big Blind**

COLLECTIONS
*Black Gods Kiss**
HebrewPunk
*The Lunacy Commission**
The Apex Book of World SF (as editor)
The Apex Book of World SF 2 (as editor)
The Apex Book of World SF 3 (as editor)

*available as a JABberwocky ebook

AN OCCUPATION
OF ANGELS

Lavie Tidhar

JABberwocky Literary Agency, Inc.

To Adam Hall, and Quiller

ONE

THE GUN WAS under the pillow and so I used it, emptying three bullets that tore through his torso before exploding, the crystal casing fragmenting and the blood inside hissing as it touched skin.

He was inhumanly large, and as I sent another bullet his way, I watched the blood—human blood, Whitehall volunteers, probably had a drop of mine in it, I hated to give blood, the needles and the smell of medical alcohol and the nurse watching you like a specimen—burn his skin away.

I turned at a sound like breaking glass but it was only a Chinese urn, Ming clay, they were suckers for Ming vases, and I turned back and shot him again, twice, once in each wing.

The blood exploded when it came in touch with the underside of his wing, and his feathers began to burn, the acrid stench making me gag.

Target reached and eliminated, or something like that. I waited as Raphael's great bulk fought to stay corporeal and lost.

Raphael's body shimmered and burnt, reducing to nothing. A halo of light expanded from it, white and clean-burning, almost reaching me.

Then his essence was gone, and it was time to get out of there.

Animal instincts taking over, I was out of the bedroom door and running, scanning for the hidden assassin who could get me at any moment, and then what would they say at the Bureau? We don't talk about our work, and if Whitehall could help it, we wouldn't be talking to each other at all, but sometimes you have to, if only to say, "Tomlin, yeah, I was with him in Tangiers, good man, imagine the East Germans cracking his network, stroke of bad luck," when what we mean is what we know in our hearts, that Tomlin might have been a good guy, but he blew the mission and there was nothing much left of him when they'd finished what they were doing and dumped him in the river, and that this could be us, me, next time, and it was pride, old stupid pride that kept me going as I ran through the mansion and out into the gardens, and continued to run until I reached the gate and opened it and jumped in a taxi and said, "Airport, please."

"Yes, Ma'am."

He hit the gas and we drove away from Raphael's House of Horrors, now minus one, at least, and I could feel myself relax and that was wrong; that was dangerous, and when things seem too easy I get worried.

"Which airline do you need?" he said.

"North Western," I said, which was the agreed code, and he said, "Really? I prefer British Airways," the whole ridiculous affair remaining ridiculous until the second you forget to use it and it's the knife in the kidney, the knife you didn't see inside the wrong newspaper, or the poison-tipped umbrella scratching your leg because you let your guard down for just one second.

"We need to get you out of the country," he said, switching to English, but he didn't take his eyes off the road and that was a good sign; the only thing that could get me out of Warsaw alive right now was a fast car on a one-way journey to the border. When you waste someone like Raphael, there are no doors, there are no holes through which you can escape, and they will hunt you. And don't even think about flying.

But— "Stop."

He wasn't telling me anything I didn't know, but there was one thing he didn't understand, and it's this: I work alone.

I relied on Control to get me a vehicle, but that was as far as it went, and so I told him to stop, and when he did I pushed him out, had to make a credible job of it, his face roughed up just enough so he would have a legitimate story to tell if he ran into them before he got back to the safe house, not that they like listening to stories, legit or otherwise, when they could just as easily kill you, or suck away the very core of you as you tried uselessly to struggle—it didn't make any difference. They'd take the core of you out and cut it into nice, neat lines and let their disciples snort the remainder of your soul through a straw. If they caught you.

I didn't intend to be caught.

I drove through a road block, and the nerves started playing up, but I was Merely Mary, I was innocent Mary Webb that day, an English teacher, thirty-one and working for VSO, and the soldier didn't look more than twenty and cheerful, and his, "Documents, please," was delivered with a smile, but still—they got Baggott in Iraq with a smile and left him with one, carved like a half-moon into his throat. I never liked the miserable bastard, but still.

The soldier at the checkpoint waved me through. I drove, foot to the accelerator, across barren cold fields.

"The guy you roughed up is going to need a doctor."

"Better that than ending up dead."

Ford waited at the rendezvous point, five kilometres from the East German border. When we're in the field, we expect our Controller to work out the bigger picture, and Ford was good, a short thin man with a balding head and a pair of reading glasses, looking like a maths teacher or a Bible salesman, you'd lose him in a crowd—which is the whole point, really.

"Roads clear," I said.

Ford looked tired. "Not without a fair bit of muscle," he said. "We even had to activate a deep-cover mole, a sleeper. I don't suppose she'll live." He said that with a soft apologetic air, coughing, and, "Anderson on the Eastern Europe Desk is rather unhappy."

Which is Ford's way of saying "Hopping mad", but I didn't care. He wouldn't say anything without a good reason, but if he meant to push me it didn't work—you can't be pushed past a certain point, and your entire being concentrates on one thing: survival.

So I said, "Can we get a move on?" and he said, "Yes," *obviously*, and *if I was in such a hurry*, and I got into the microlight, I'd sit Ford behind me; he was good but I wanted to survive, and when you do, there is only one person you trust.

I'd slid into a pair of overalls and now speeded up along the track road and then we were in the air and climbing, and I was grateful for the overalls. It gets cold quickly up there, and you need the insulation.

Flying blind and in fear of angels, the action is a strange dance, trying to keep between the two realms. There's the human one below, the realm of the *Sluzba Bezpieczeństwa* and *Stasi*, of dank cells and rats and beatings, blood in water—but I wasn't going to think about that, I was going to think ahead, to safety, to getting away with it.

Just don't fly too high.

There's the human realm, and then there's the heavenly one where the winged predators ruled.

We flew over the border into East Germany and I consulted the map as I let the microlight glide, unassisted, then grabbed hold of the bars again and swooped north, Ford behind me— and I knew the thing with Raphael had been serious, they wouldn't let someone like Ford out of bed for less than a revolution, nukes, or angels.

And they wouldn't have asked for me.

Racing through cold clear air, waiting, the nerves on edge, piano wires stretched to snap.

But still we weren't disturbed; the air remained clear and bright, no sign of unfriendly visitations, no sign of wings, and the ground, as much of it as I could see, remained clear of their agents, and we flew until I could smell the sea cutting like a blade against skin, salty and smoky at the same time, and a flare went up and I made an awkward landing, bumpy, but we rode it until the microlight stopped and I got out and, not waiting for Ford to unstrap himself, jumped onto the deck of the boat without ceremony and commandeered the ladies bathrooms.

It gets *cold* up there.

At 04:15 we touched Dover and at 05:30 I was back in London, alive, and the adrenaline wearing off and needing release, and I went to find Ben and woke him up, which he didn't mind at all.

TWO

THERE WAS CHANTING at Trafalgar Square, protesters walking up and down with plaques that said WHAT DO THEY WANT? THEY WANT POWER and A MANIFESTATION TOO MANY, and it started to rain, not the usual kind of drizzle but the temporary, great outpouring of the sky, and I cursed and flagged down a cab.

I'd been back in London for more than a month and I'd been getting restless.

They know that, and they play with you, trying to make sure that when they really need you, when they can't find another poor fool, they have you. "Killarney," they say, in their cold quiet rooms. "Just the ticket, Killarney. The girl who won't turn down the mission everyone else has turned down, and you know why, old boy? It's pride, old obstinate pride because she wants to be the person who does it and gets it done and comes out again."

I got off a few streets before the Bureau—habit, really—and walked the rest of the way to the squat, brown office building and went inside, and the heaters didn't work.

"You might want to come round when you have a moment." Oldham had called me at nine in the morning; outside the windows it still looked like midnight.

"Anything important?"

"Oh, not really, dear girl, might have something for you, never know."

"How's the kid?"

"Doing well. She's going to Oxford next year. Listen, Killarney, must dash, pop round if you have some time."

Click.

They wanted me and they didn't want to let on. You don't get calls from Oldham or anybody else at the Bureau asking you to come in unless they need you—but they were playing it very cool, and that had me worried.

I walked down the corridors and ran into Berlyne coming out of the cipher room. "Meta," went the speakers inside, a voice stretched almost to its breaking point, "Tron," the sequence repeating, "Meta, Tron, Meta Tron, Metatron," and I had to snap out of the hypnotic quality of the recording, and Berlyne shut the door, cutting off the noise.

"Metatron up to something?"

Berlyne just looked at me. "Metatron is *always* up to something, Killarney. Every Archangel is, at any given moment, up to something. Following which, unpleasant things inevitably happen." It seemed to cheer him up.

"So what's going on, Berlyne? Any idea why I was called in?"

"Were you called in? Can't imagine why. Place is as dead as a church. And the heaters don't work." He rubbed his hands together as if warmed by the thought. "Might be an idea for you to see Turner though."

I left him there, still rubbing his hands, and I went to find Turner, thinking how casual, how *debonair* everyone suddenly seemed round here.

Malcolm, Turner's personal assistant, was outside the door smoking a cigarette. He grinned and proffered his BH pack when I walked up.

I waved it away.

"Is he busy?"

"Be done in a minute. Meeting."

"Anything I should know about?" I was getting tired of asking questions, but I was edgy again, the fake calm serving to heighten my awareness that something was being put into motion behind the scenes and when it came out, more likely than not, I would be caught in the avalanche.

Malcolm shrugged. "Nothing much happening this time of year. We're trying to get someone to come in and fix the heating but the union is on strike, can you believe it?"

I couldn't believe any of it. Malcolm finished his cigarette and knocked on the door. "She's here," he called, and opened the door for me, closing it behind me softly and leaving me in the room.

Turner perched at the end of an ancient desk like an owl in mourning. Rain streaked down the naked windows. A small, rusting electric heater, dark red like the colour of a used bullet, lay at his feet.

"Sit down."

They say his wife left him and then drowned herself, and that he never forgave himself, or her. Whatever the reason, Turner is cold; if you froze him in ice for a hundred years and then defrosted him, he'd just come alive again like those fish they found in Antarctica.

"Might have a little job for you," Turner said. He rubbed his hands in front of the electric bars.

"So I keep hearing." A flash of lightning outside, followed by thunder.

"We lost someone in Paris." He said it without emotion, as if offering a biscuit at tea time. "We'd like you to get him back."

I was going to say, "What do you mean, you lost someone in Paris?" but of course I didn't because the Bureau doesn't, *doesn't* lose people, and what he meant was that, whoever the poor bastard was, he was probably dead by now, that or working for the other side.

"Who?"

He pulled out a thick file from the cabinet behind the table and lay it in front of me. It opened onto a series of black and white photographs showing a man in his middle thirties, pasty complexion, thick black moustache, round glasses, and I committed his face to memory because, from now on, that would be a face I'd be looking for.

"It's nothing drastic, Killarney," Turner said, and I watched the reflection of the heated bars twist and melt in his glasses. "A man by the name of Eldershott. An academic, really." He said that almost apologetically. "Cryptography, though you couldn't tell to look at him, good solid work but he wasn't that important. He was on holiday in Paris, alone—he's not married, seemed to lead a quiet life—and Paris is clean; it's friendly ground. Then he just…disappeared." His hands raised in a shrug, palms open upwards as if to say, *Such inconvenience.*

"We had a couple of people watching him, and they swore he never left the hotel all night."

Playing a hunch: "What did the hotel say?"

Turner looked at me accusingly. "The hotel said he never checked in that night."

We locked stares. I broke contact first. I said, "KGB?"

Not *SDECE*, the French are friendlies, and not the Chinese, either—they don't have angels, and since the Coming they mainly stick to themselves.

Turner smiled. The owl shaking its wings. "We were hoping you could find that out for us."

They were making every effort to put me at ease, and Paris, for Christ's sake, that was almost home ground, and a part of you thinking maybe this one will be a breeze—which is when you cross that line, the one that keeps you alive. Keep thinking like that and the next thing is your brain is splattered on a pavement, a rifle shot hitting home, just like they did to Bergman, Bergman in Barcelona with the shorts and the beach hat and the funny sunglasses, Bergman because he thought, *this one's going to be easy.*

"You'll be doing us a favour," Turner said, "Paris, you'll be there in half a day, root round the city for a bit, see if you can dig up Eldershott from wherever he got himself to, get back." He shrugged again, offered me half a smile like a sliver of ice. "You could turn it down, of course."

Of course I could turn it down. We can always turn down the mission, and he'd only mentioned it to see if I'd take the bait, by offering me an exit line on what he tried so hard to describe as a routine mission. Only you didn't just lose your own people on your home turf, and I knew that, and he knew that I knew.

And I didn't care. It was a mission, and I was going to take it. Just like he knew I would.

in from Place Pigalle keeping the rooms occupied, if only for an hour at a time, and someone probably dealing a little Algerian hash in the back.

Traffic was hell and the rain fell down like a warning, and I went round the obelisk twice before finally getting onto the road I needed. I was going to make sure I didn't go anywhere near Notre Dame; you never want to expose yourself unnecessarily to one of them.

I had left Turner at his office, then wandered over to Provisions.

"Ah, Killareny." Dobson, mousy and twee in a dark suit that looked like it had been stolen from a coffin. He pulled out a file and passed it to me.

"Anna Krojer," he said, "age twenty-seven, German, spent the last year in London studying textile design. Going to Paris on holiday before returning home. I expect you to have memorised the dossier by the time you get to Paris."

"When do I leave?"

"We were able to fit you in on the next flight." He came from round the counter. "That's in two hours." Mousy moustache quivering. "We're also going to need to arm you."

That wasn't entirely unexpected, but I didn't like it. I don't usually carry guns; guns make you think they're the answer and when they're not there and you don't know what to do, you're finished. I prefer relying on instinct and my head, not a useless piece of metal. I used it last time but only because it was already there for me, and that was an assassination and you can't kill one of those bastards without a whole clip of bullets pumped up with blood, that or a bloody nuke.

"No," I said, "thank you," and he didn't suggest it again, but it made me nervous because, unless angels are involved,

I mean directly involved, they wouldn't have suggested it, and if angels were involved, then this mission was set up a hell of a long time in advance, and they were pretending that it wasn't.

"Anything else?" Dobson said, and what he meant was: what final arrangements do you want to make if the executive is lost in the field? I thought about it, and I'd end up doing what I always did, which was to send a single red rose to Ben. *In the event of the shadow executive failing to complete the mission.*

"Sign here and…here."

There was a car outside and I hurried in, getting in the front next to Marshall who drove me cheerfully through the rain to Heathrow.

"Have a good time in Paris." He'd saluted me with two fingers to the temple and driven off, still whistling.

"Do you have a double room?" I went into three hotels before I got here, acting just like a tourist would when looking for a cheap room. I was clean; I didn't have a tail when I left the airport, but I didn't know enough, and when I'm in the field, nowhere is friendly ground. Not knowing the full extent of the mission doesn't worry me; in fact I prefer it that way; if the executive in the field knew too much about the mission she would begin worrying. I prefer relying on myself to figure it out without getting killed, but what I didn't like was that they had tried very hard to make it sound routine, and they had lied. "When was the reservation made?" I'd asked the clerk at Avis, and she'd said the call had come through the day before. Which meant this was no holiday away in Paris, no simple missing person job; this was the real thing and all bets were off.

"Let me see." The hotel clerk spoke a careful English. Beard, deep set eyes, fingers with the nails chewed clean flicking through a register. "Yes I think we can give you one, is it for you and…I see."

I gave him the passport, the Anna Krojer one, and paid in cash for two nights in advance. This wasn't the sort of place that took credit cards.

The room was on the second floor, a climb up the narrow spiral stairs and I had the room facing the street, a double, complete with rusting sink and mildewed shower. It would do. I don't like singles—there is less room to manoeuvre.

This wasn't the hotel he'd stayed in; that was the third one I'd tried, and I only went in to see the floor plan and to check the room Eldershott was supposed to have stayed in, which wasn't much different from the one I was currently in: springy bed, chipped sink, a mouse slinking out of the wainscoting as if embarrassed to be seen in such surroundings. I knew how it felt.

He'd had a double, too, and I wondered who he had tried to bring back there with him; I didn't think he'd stayed a stone's throw away from the red light district that was Place Pigalle without reason.

I opened the window and looked down. I could jump if I needed to; it wasn't too high unless you lost your nerve, and then you'd be finished anyway. The dossier said he had stayed at the hotel for three nights—the minders didn't seen him leave on the fourth one, and the hotel said he never checked in again after going out at night, but how or why or when, they were vague about. The dossier added that it didn't seem like a deliberate smokescreen operation, just French uncooperativeness.

I had to find Eldershott, and I had a feeling the answer lay just down the road, where the street stalls and the clothes shops gave way to peepshows and cabarets.

FOUR

BLOOD POURED FROM her side where I plunged
the knife between the ribs, and still she struck at me, her
kick failing to connect, and I smashed her nose with the
palm of my left hand, driving the broken bone deep, towards
the brain.

The organism taking over when you're attacked, feral
instincts and the burning desire to kill, and to live, and I guess
that's why I do what I do and let other people do nine to five
or fix the taps when they leak; you only really live when your
life is threatened.

Her eyes rolled and she fell down on the floor with a soft
whoop, blood smearing her naked skin. She wore a thong and
not much else, but she must have had instructions, *kill on
sight* or something similar, because she'd jumped me as soon as
I was alone, trailing me to the ladies' bathrooms and attempting a knife attack, and I hit her, kicking the knife from her
hand and grabbing it before it fell, and driving it into her
with one motion, and that's the benefit of *krav maga* over the
other martial art forms, Kung Fu and karate and Tai Kwan
Do, that it doesn't teach you philosophy, it teaches you to kill
with whatever you have to hand and with everything else, too.

The Israelis had developed it for their Mossad agents, and we'd borrowed it from them.

Someone tried the door and I blocked it.

"Cleaning!"

The whole thing only took a moment; I hadn't been in Paris twenty-four hours and already there was a corpse and I had to do something about it.

There were two cubicles and I put her into the one furthest from the door, propping her on the seat, white girl, petite, dark hair that looked like it might have been professionally dyed. Her hand flopped down and exposed a tattoo on her wrist: an inverted swastika inked in red with a spread wing on each side. I hadn't seen that before and it was making me worried, suggesting the opposition were new. Unknown meant unpredictable in this business, a different kind of dangerous.

I left the toilet cover up, positioning her so that the blood ebbed into the bowl below, turning the water red. I used toilet paper to wipe blood from the floor—I'd have to take the knife with me—and I closed the door on her and locked it from the outside, moving the screw with the knife until it clicked.

"Champagne?" He'd obviously thought I worked there and had been trying to impress me, the left hand in his pocket probably hiding the pale band where the wedding ring had been just before he'd come into the club.

Le Minou Rose. The Pink Pussycat. It was the fourth one I'd gone into and already I was getting sick of it, the smoke and the dim lighting and the men in cheap suits and the girls who served them. The wealth of the clientele diminished with each nightclub and this one was positively budget, and packed.

"No, thank you."

It was easier to talk to the bartenders. To talk to a girl I'd have to hire her, and that would raise questions, and she might not want to talk however much I offered her. I slid the photo across the counter and he nodded, once, and took the note I gave him and turned away.

Then I'd gone to the loo and the girl had attacked me and suddenly everything had changed.

There were two options and I much preferred the first. That by asking the bartender about Eldershott, I had triggered an immediate response, and that was all there was to it. I didn't like the other option: that they knew who I was, that somewhere there was a picture of me and that they circulated it with clear-cut instructions. They wouldn't have my name but the fact is that someone, somewhere, could have managed to snap the right picture and that I was now a major target for the opposition, and I had to get out of there.

I left the bathrooms and closed the door behind me, jamming it. I needed time. I was going with the first option, for the moment.

I stood in the entrance to the club's interior and examined the room, looking for potential assassins.

I had to get the information, had to track down Eldershott, and I knew this was the place, this was the focal point, and they were watching it, and if they didn't know who I was they would soon, if I didn't make it out of there—but I couldn't run. I was the ferret dumped into the chicken coop to stir everything up.

I went back to the bar. The same bartender was still there.

Still going with option one.

"Thought we'd continue our chat."

He shrugged, soundlessly.

"Can you tell me where I might find him?" I slipped a second note towards him, larger than the first. I was perched on the bar, scanning the crowd.

The bartender seemed to think it through.

I added two more notes and straightened them on the counter.

He jerked his head, once, and the notes disappeared.

I waited as he served a customer, rang it through, then left the bar (there was a whispered argument with a replacement, and I suspected money changed hands again). I got up and followed him through the corridors and out of the back, a fire escape and a freezing alley where the stench of fermented garbage permeated everything.

"Who are you?" he said, and he spoke English, not French, which should have warned me plenty. It was Northern Irish.

He had the voice of a smoker, but he didn't make a move to take out a cigarette, just stood there calmly and watched me, waiting for me to give him a good enough reason to trust me. I wanted to know who he worked for.

The Anna Krojer identity wasn't going to do me much good, not anymore, and not with this man. So I said, "I think Eldershott might be in trouble," and watched his face as I said it, and he was good, not a muscle moved but his eyes shifted, only a fraction, but I knew he recognised the name and that this was more than a random bar the target had happened to wander into, this was a relationship, so I waited, baiting him with the name to get a response.

"Who are you?" he said again, but from the tone it was evident he wasn't going to fight the point; he knew he wouldn't get an answer he could do anything with. So instead of an answer, I took out three new notes, American, knowing the bloodsuckers in Accounts were going to raise hell about it, and after a moment's pause he took them and made them disappear. "I'm retired," he said. His sudden grin was warm, lighting up his face. I said, "IRA?" and he shrugged. "Once. You're what, MI6?"

"No."

He shrugged again, saying it didn't matter to him. "I thought someone would show up sooner or later."

I thought he could have been part of the opposition, but he was just a freelancer. "Tell me about Eldershott," I said.

"There's a girl," he said. "Sophie." Then, "Sophie Stockard. John took a real shine to her. The rule in the club is no touching, no soliciting. But what the *girls* do outside the club is their business."

I registered the sudden nervousness, now that he was committed, now that he was telling me this. Subtle signs, a narrowing of the eyes, the left hand making a circling motion over the thumb. And the name, *John*, not Eldershott, and I thought, *There are deeper connections here.* A larger picture of which I was ignorant.

He gave me an address and the hair at the back of my neck rose because it was the Quartier Latin, almost in view of the cathedral, and I knew, then, that this was something to do with the angels, something to do with *Metatron* specifically, and it was going to be a mess, no matter how you looked at it when you picked up the broken, bloodied pieces.

He was going to sing like a canary down the mine, I knew that; he was going to open up and let me have it, his life story if I wanted it; he seemed willing enough to talk when the price was right. I was reaching into a pocket for more contributions to his retirement fund and I should have been paying attention, but I wasn't.

He must have known something was off, the way he twitched, suddenly, and looked to the side, but it was too late and the bullet penetrated his skull, just a normal run of the mill metal slug, nothing fancy like a blood bullet, and he went down like a car crash and stayed there, twitching a moment longer before dying.

FIVE

IT WAS A long distance shot, a sniper and a good one, and I was behind my nameless Irish bartender even as he fell, trying to shield myself from any more bullets that might come flying out of the darkness, though the corpse wouldn't be much help against a sniper rifle.

I hugged the wall, hiding in the shadow, waiting—another shot, inches from my face, throwing plaster in the air, stinging my cheek—somehow it felt like a goodbye. I scanned the rooftops, saw nothing.

Breathing heavily, waiting—they had already tried to kill me once tonight—but nothing came and the bartender was still dead at my feet and I had to get out of there. I worked my way around and down the alley and no-one shot at me. I followed it until it rejoined the main thoroughfare where bright neon lights lit up the night and busty girls tried to tempt bedraggled men into passing the time together—how much time depending purely on the price.

Fear, because someone didn't want me to find Eldershott and was actively trying to kill me before I did; fear, because they could have had my photo by now, they would know what I looked like and there is only so much you can do to change your appearance, the best thing is to get lost in the crowd, anonymous clothes and anonymous faces and stick to where other people are and blend in with them.

Fear, and the organism rearing to change the situation, to hunt and not be hunted, and fear because there were too many unknowns, but now I had a name and an address to match to one of them: Sophie Stockard. I hoped she was still alive.

Barbes Rochechouart. The station was crowded and stank of piss. I took the train towards Porte d'Orleans and sat down, and practiced controlling my breathing. After a while I felt calmer.

I reached Saint Michel and stepped out into cold, fresh air, the scent of roasting chestnuts and *Sandwich Grec*, and the tang of angel on the wind.

Notre Dame was hidden behind restaurants, and I dreaded the thought of being close enough to see as well as feel the power of the Archangel. All it would take were a few steps, just enough to reach the river, and then the cathedral would be in a direct line of sight.

The Quartier Latin was bewitched, encased in glamour. Intensely handsome couples walked, laughing, arms entwined. Music played, manically, in the street, here a lonely guitar, there a group of Algerians playing loud, French Hip Hop. They danced to the tune, hard, sweat pouring down their skins. They seemed possessed, driven by the presence of the corrupting divine. All around, the competing scents of cooking foods wafted on the wind, their smells like a physical, overwhelming presence.

Everything, if you spent long enough at the Latin Quarter, was overwhelming.

I hurried down the avenues, trying to remain focused. Breathing, the heart beating, the blood spreading through my body as if trying to escape it, and I concentrated on the girl, Sophie Stockard. When I reached the narrow alleyway and the number the bartender had given me, there was a light in the second-floor window, and I thought, *Please, please let her still be alive.*

She was mad to live here, this close to the Archangel, and I felt the nerves tingling as I knocked on the front door, found it unlocked and went into the building.

It was dark inside, with the smell of cheap rented flats, hard detergents that do not cover up the stench of accumulated years. "Sophie?" I called out, feeling for the stairs (carpet, thick and slimy to the touch) and beginning to climb.

Who are you?

I was getting tired of being asked that question, and for a second, terrified; it echoed in my head, in a language I didn't know and yet understood. And again, the force of the thought almost throwing me back against the stairs, *who are you?*

I could sense more than words, as if whoever spoke was trying to find out the answer from me through stealth, like fingers easing into my mind and grasping.

Breathe. Breathe. Concentrate. The mission, and Sophie, I was focusing on Sophie, Sophie and breathing, controlling, Sophie, Sophie.

And then I could see her, as I reached the top of the stairs and stood on the landing.

She was standing by the window, an open window through which the full moon could be seen rising behind the turrets of Notre Dame. Sophie Stockard stood in a nightgown like those worn by hospital patients, with nothing underneath. Her bare feet seemed frozen to the ground; there were icicles around them, like diamond encampments. She had a dancer's body, lithe and thin.

He suffers. There was laughter in the voice. Her eyes were grey. She examined me for a long moment. I didn't know what to think.

"Eldershott?" I said.

Her eyes lost their focus for a second. Then the intensity was back. Behind her, I could see Metatron's gigantic appendages bursting out of the broken windows of the cathedral, thrashing in the air.

Johnny. Johnny. Johnny. Her voice echoed and pounded me. It sounded like a wail, but all that time she didn't move, didn't shift her gaze from me, only this voice coming outvof nothing and into my head and bloody Metatron and the full moon and I thought, *This is it, this is where death comes.*

"Johnny was good to me," she said. It took me a moment to realise she had spoken that out loud. She spoke French with a southerner accent. Her voice had a petulant tone. She said, "He was a gentleman."

"There are so few," I said, and thought she might smile, but she didn't.

Johnny is gone. The voice came from her, too, I knew that, and yet it wasn't. Was she channelling? If she was, I didn't want to meet the thing on the other end.

"Johnny said we could go to the Bahamas," Sophie said. "He said he would buy us a house with coconut trees and I would only dance for him."

Fool, said the voice, and yet it had a mournful tone. And again, with that awful laughter, *He dies.*

I tried to move towards her but my perspective changed; the walls were melting around me in a swampy green; the ceiling dribbled and fell in drops to the floor, and where I stepped in it, it turned to blood.

"Who is dying?" I said. My voice came out thick and indistinct, as if I were speaking through water. The air felt alive around me, elastic, pliable.

"We were going to be so happy. Only he had to go off in a hurry. He said it will solve all of our problems. That this was a once-in-a-lifetime opportunity, like something from heaven."

Shut up! The voice, raging, and I was falling into a vortex of dark colours, sucked into the floor.

Concentrate. Breathe. Control.

I opened my eyes and I was back in the hallway, standing the same distance away from Sophie. I didn't like what she was saying. An opportunity from heaven. I wondered if Eldershott knew what he had got himself into. I wondered if I did.

Can you feel it? said that awful voice, and there was terrible delight in it.

And I could, all of a sudden. Like an explosion of pain, humiliation, torment, fear—he was like a bear wounded and still struggling as its death was being carried out.

I could feel it, and it was terrible. And I watched it happen, and was unable to turn away.

There were cracks in the cathedral now and, as I watched, Metatron's body shuddered once, fracturing the entire building, and then he was gone, and Sophie turned around to me and the voice laughed and then she jumped out of the window.

It took me a fraction of a second to get to the window, but she was already in the air and then she disappeared, just disappeared in a final distortion that seemed to shake the world one last time, and she was gone and I was standing in an ordinary house, looking at an ordinary street, and Metatron's gigantic corpse flopped lifelessly through the broken windows of Notre Dame.

SIX

"TWO PIECES OF luggage are permanently lost."

I was standing by the public phones, close to the *Shakespeare and Co* bookshop, looking over at Notre Dame. The place had an abandoned aura, the charm of the Archangel banished. It felt human again.

I didn't bother with a cipher, and one public phone is the same as the next. It was as secure as anything else right then and I was in a hurry.

"I am terribly sad to hear of your trouble." It was Berlyne again, on duty in the communications room. "How may we compensate you?"

Two pieces of luggage: a dancer and a bartender. "Oh," I said, as if the thought has just struck me, "there was a third piece of luggage I lost recently. It was very precious. Heavenly."

And an Archangel. Paris was yet again without a Presence. "I see."

"I want a representative of the company to meet me in person," I said. "As soon as possible."

It took him quite a while to get back to me. In the square in front of the cathedral there was a crowd, held back less by police tape and more by several large policemen. I wondered how they were going to conduct this particular investigation.

"Tomorrow morning." he said.

"Now look—" I started, but he interrupted me to give me an address. "You can stay there tonight, if you like. On the company expense. We hope you accept it as partial compensation for your troubles."

He hung up.

I got a cab. Someone would have to inform Avis where I'd left the car and arrange for it to be returned. Right now, it seemed the safest bet for Anna Krojer to disappear.

The address I was given turned out to be a Moroccan restaurant near the Gare du Nord. As I went through the doors the smell of cooking hit me, and I realised how hungry I was, and how tired.

The organism needed to recharge, demanded fuel.

A short, olive-skinned man with a bald patch hurried towards me with open arms. "Mademoiselle! Please, come in, sit, please!" He ushered me to a corner table and I sat down, facing the door.

"My eldest son's wife." He said it with another big show of hands, speaking to the diners who were paying him no attention.

"Mohammed Giza," he said in a low voice, shaking my hand. "Don't worry, you're safe here."

"Could I have some food?"

He must have seen how hungry I was. "Of course."

In moments, a large tray of couscous with roast lamb and a thick vegetable stew was deposited on my table, together with a carafe of water.

Recharging. I concentrated on the taste of the food, drank glasses of water.

They brought me another carafe, and more lamb.

When I felt as if I were human again I sat back, and after a couple of minutes a small pot of thick, dark coffee was put in front of me, together with a plate of honeyed pastry.

I chewed on the sweet, flaking pastry and drank coffee and felt my mind return to something resembling functionality.

I had a cryptographer missing. I had his girlfriend, who seemed to have strange powers and two minds, and who was also, though more recently, missing. Finally, I had a dead Archangel—the second in as many months.

Could they be linked? Could my assassination of Raphael have played a part, however remotely, in Metatron's killing?

I didn't like the picture I was coming up with. I thought, *They'd better send me someone I can work with; not Reynolds, he could get me killed; not Ramsey—he once let an executive fall to the Russians because he wanted to feed them misinformation—not Feltham, she has more dead Executives than a barrel of puppies.* But there was nothing to gain by sitting there worrying about it, so I just sipped my coffee and watched the door and tried to put the pieces together and couldn't.

I slept badly that night. Visions of the Archangels kept plaguing my dreams. Raphael's coarse, bloated figure as the blood hit it and consumed it; the monstrosity that was Metatron, shuddering in its body of ancient bricks, the way his huge form ceased to move, his limbs hanging limply from the broken windows.

And through it all, the face of Eldershott swam in my mind, the moustache and glasses hiding an unreadable expression.

Eldershott, and, as I dreamt, those other eyes returned to haunt me, Sophie's grey, calm eyes and the inhuman voice that kept calling my name, *Killarney, Killarney, Killarney...*

"Killarney!"

Darkness. Pale light trying to edge in through the narrow windows. Foggy outside. The smell of raw garlic.

Seago was leaning against the door, hands folded on his chest like a neatly ironed shirt. Seago. I'd worked with him in Lebanon and the Gambia, and though he was a miserable bastard, he knew what he was doing, and he always got you out alive. If he could. He'd lost Pickin in the Iran thing, but everyone knew Pickin was already on his last leg, and he lost it when the *Savak* men came for him that final time. Went out in style, though—they said the explosion had demolished an entire street, though I suspect that was an exaggeration.

"When did you get here?"

Seago took out a packet of cigarettes, *Gauloises*, how's that for a bit of local colour? Not that Seago had any colour; he was as pale as a chalk mine, and as deep.

"Three days ago."

"What?" *He's been here longer than I have.* My suspicions were confirmed: they'd been building up to this for a long time and played me for the part, running me all the way, Turner, with his cold blood and his shrug that said, *You could say no,* knowing I wouldn't.

Seago saw my expression. "Didn't they tell you I was going to be your controller? I don't know what Turner was thinking."

I wondered if he was telling me the truth, but I let it pass. "Seago," I said, "go and light that cigarette outside. I'll meet you downstairs in five minutes."

He did, and I got up, went for a pee, brushed my teeth, got dressed, did all the normal things you do when you get up, regardless of espionage, the Cold War or Archangels.

It was a safe house, at least for now.

When I got downstairs, the restaurant was closed. Seago sat alone at a corner table, smoking. The stub of one cigarette was already in the ashtray.

"Coffee?" He didn't wait for an answer but poured the dark liquid into a small china cup and another helping into his own.

I sat opposite him, stretching out my legs. When I drank, the coffee rushed through my system, the organism gearing up, charged and ready to fight again. It felt good.

"Look, Killarney," Seago said, "I want you to know I didn't have anything to do with not briefing you beforehand. In fact, I think it was irresponsible. Turner assured me they had you for this mission over two weeks ago."

That was Seago, and I was grateful I had someone in local Control who I could trust to tell me the truth, if not *all* of it.

"So what's going on, Seago? Last night I saw an Archangel die, not to mention two people, one of whom I killed. This isn't a spy game, this is a God-damned full-on military assault."

"Killarney." He sipped his coffee. Instead of an answer, he offered me a question. "How do you think you got out of Warsaw?"

The same question had been bothering me. I levelled a stare at him. He looked back without any expression, ticked points on his fingers. "There was no-one guarding Raphael," he said. "Our mole planted the gun under the pillow without being detected. The Stasi didn't get you. And you and Ford had a clear run all the way home. Convenient?"

"Lucky," I said—admitted. Knowing there was no such thing as luck in this game.

He nodded. "It was a perfect mission. Perfectly planned, perfectly executed." He offered me a smile around his cigarette. "But there's no such thing as a perfect mission."

"So what was it?" I said. I was tired of sparring, and of partial truths, and we always get that way, deep into a mission and we're feeling our way in the dark. "You tell me."

"I don't know," he said. He also sounded tired. "It's one of the things we're trying to find out. We think someone is arranging the assassinations of the Archangels. We suspect they used the Bureau to do that with the Raphael killing, and we have to ask ourselves: who has the power to do something like that?" He lit another cigarette, a third, and the earlier one was still burning. I suddenly realised how weary he was, and how frightened Whitehall must be to find the opposition—whoever they were—had the power to reach so closely into our most secret places.

"You need to find Eldershott. He was one of our cryptographers with an interest in angels. He specialised in the field of angelic communication. *Highly* specialised." If it was a bad pun he didn't let on. "And now he's gone, and we've killed Raphael and someone killed Metatron, and now both the East and the West are one Archangel down and, as you said, Killareny, this isn't a cold war anymore; it's heating up and we have to stop it."

It was a long speech for him and it put me in the picture as much as they wanted to, which meant there were a hell of a lot of questions I didn't have answers for.

"Now I'd like your report."

I told Seago everything, about finding Sophie and feeling Metatron die. He grimaced at that.

"You weren't the only one to feel it," he said. "I was in Bastille when it happened, like a tremor in the earth that you felt in your head. It was madness, after that."

I waited him out. I drank more coffee. The empty restaurant was quiet.

"We need you to leave Paris," he said at last. "We don't know who's behind this but let's put it this way, there can't be too many powers with the ability to pull it off."

The Americans were out. They'd meddled as much as they could in Europe, but they had a Church-led government and they wouldn't dare touch an angel, let alone an Archangel. If anything, they'd be worried someone was going to make an attempt on one of their own. The Chinese—possibly, there were no angels in China that we knew about, and they didn't like the Russians; but I doubted they had the kind of muscle to pull this off. It could have been another Archangel, but they have never, in all the thirty-five years since the Coming, killed one of their own. Humans, yes, when the need arose, but never each other.

"You suspect the Russians?"

He spoke carefully. "We think they might be behind this. Eldershott was approached by an agent of the KGB's Fourth Directorate the month before he disappeared."

Shit.

Angels were bad but the Fourth Directorate were worse, and I knew where this was heading even before he said it, and I cursed him inside, thinking, *This is where it* really *gets hard.*

They were sending me to Moscow.

SEVEN

SNOW COVERED THE empty streets like a crystalline layer of dust. I drove through the streets of Moscow and wondered how much longer I could stay alive.

Name, Marija Zita, thirty-five, hair a dark brown and cut short. Serb, with the kind of accent one associates with eating razorblades. Dress, business suit, a good cut but obviously worn, and I was shown through at the border post from Norway, you couldn't get any more remote than that, and I was inside the Soviet Union and on my way to a rendezvous with a very messy outcome, if I knew anything at all.

I picked up a flight at Leningrad and got off at Moscow in the middle of the night, the darkest part that comes an hour or two before sunrise, when everyone human was asleep and even the birds were still.

The car was waiting for me and I drove to the university, Moscow's People's Friendship University, and I thought, *They must have every bloody room of this place bugged, and who the hell came up with the idea, and I bet Seago sleeps somewhere decent.*

I got there at four thirty in the morning. A sleepy-looking Chinese man let me in and pointed me to a room. I didn't think he was one of ours, so he could have been working for the PRC, which meant this was massive; if Whitehall was talking to Beijing, then all hell was riding on this mission, and so far I had nothing but two dead bodies and my own, which was almost keeling over.

I slept for four hours, getting up at nine and putting on a comfortable outfit, more third-world student than business-woman, and got back in the car.

Even from a distance, you could see Gor'el, and feel him even before you saw anything. His gigantic bulk stuck out of the smashed windows of the GUM department store, and beside him, Sorel's own monstrous appendages stuck out of St. Basil's Church.

Two of the three.

Then I went round a corner and the Kremlin came into view, and the power of the three Archangels hit me like a punch to the ribs and I almost swerved because the Archangel Michael was in residence, and the body of the Kremlin looked like it was suddenly made of pliable mud as Michael hid his inhuman bulk inside it.

Red Square. AKA The Square of the Three Archangels.

It was a curious sensation, but once you set foot in the Square itself, the awesome influence of the Archangels almost ceased as if the three somehow cancelled each other out.

I met Seago by Lenin's tomb. A queue snaked outside into the cold; maybe they wanted to make sure he was dead.

Seago looked almost as bad as Lenin.

"He's being held inside," he said.

I should have known—and it was suddenly much colder.

"We want you to get into Lubyanka."

Being this close to the Archangels made me nervous, but not nearly as much as the thought of Lubyanka did; Gordon had died there, and Philpot had been as good as dead when they'd sent him back like an unwanted holiday present still wrapped up in blood and puss.

I'd been inside, once. And I'd got out. I guess that made me somewhat unique.

"How do you know?" It was blunt, but I was getting tired of being kept in the dark, and restless to finish what I had to do and get out of there as soon as was humanly possible.

There was the sound of a blast and a new crack appeared in GUM's side.

"The angels are restless," Seago said, and I knew that was all the answer I was going to get. The Bureau was playing the game and playing me, which was fine, but now I didn't know if they were being played themselves, and that was a thought I didn't like.

"How do I get in?" I asked, and Seago handed me one of his brown envelopes and then went to join the queue to see Lenin.

I was glad to be away from there, away from the Archangels. I wondered if one or more of them would be executed as their counterparts in Poland and France had been, if they'd find another human patsy to pull the trigger.

Discovered I didn't much care.

Lubyanka was a short way away by foot from Red Square, and I stood in the shadow of an adjacent building and watched that great black cube that sucked in life and left only broken, useless bones. Light and sound seemed to diminish around it.

No wonder we had so much trouble keeping the Russians at bay; they had guardian angels coming out of their arses, and they had Azrael inside Lubyanka. No-one had ever admitted to seeing him after the first day of the Coming. They say he loved Lubyanka too much to leave; it provided him with everything he wished for.

I got rid of the brown envelope in the first ten minutes, reading it in the public bathrooms and tearing and flushing the papers immediately afterwards.

So they knew where Eldershott was being held. Interesting. Something didn't gel, but I wasn't sure what it was. The Bureau seemed simultaneously dead worried and quietly confident. If they had this kind of information, they needn't have worried and the fact they did helped to unbalance me, and I began taking short, controlled breaths as I examined the building in more detail, noting hidden guards, possible entries, all the time the thought running through my head that something wasn't right.

Time was a factor. Seago didn't say it outright, he knew better than to push me, but I could tell it in his face, the way he acted, and it came through in the notes, *objective: get captive out at all cost, and do it bloody quickly*, or words to that effect, and I thought I'd better get a move on, and when a car pulled up I grabbed a metal bar. It was a rusting window frame, broken, and I began smashing the car whilst the guy inside it started screaming at me. They came out of the building then, as I'd known they would, six or seven of them, young, dressed all in black, no insignia, like the building. They had truncheons in their hands, and guns, and they tried to grab me and I tried to fight, forgetting everything I knew and just using street punches, and they had me pinned to the ground and then I was being taken inside and, as they were carrying me, something heavy connected with the back of my head and I lost consciousness.

EIGHT

WHEN TORTURED, EVERY person has a breaking point, an edge at the end of consciousness beyond which they're lost. A good torturer knows this and tries to keep you on the safe side of the chasm. They can't use you when you break.

When tortured, there are two types of people. Those who crack before getting to the chasm, and those who can try and ride the line that separates tortured sanity from madness, those who find within themselves a core of—of *stubbornness*, perhaps—that makes them try and defy the torturer until they are beyond the chasm, at which point they are no longer useful as information sources—or anything else.

A good torturer knows this.

I was sitting in a small, windowless room. Sitting on a metal chair, my hands and feet tied to the chair with rough, metal wires that dug into the flesh. There was a bucket of water in the corner.

"Pochemu Vy napadali na avtomobil?" She was in her middle thirties, white lab coat and soft, German-made shoes that must have cost a month's salary for the average comrade.

Why were you attacking the car?

"Ja ne ponimaju." I tried to sound frightened, which wasn't difficult. She was a professional, and they are the people we usually encounter if we're unlucky enough, or stupid enough, to fall into the hands of the opposition—at that level you don't get many amateurs.

I don't understand.

They didn't know who I was, and it would take them too long to connect Marija Zita with Anna Krojer; as far as she was concerned, I was a Serb student who'd suddenly gone a little crazy, but they were taking no chances, and I was counting on that to get me into Lubyanka, and it had worked, and now came the hard part.

Someone somewhere flipped a switch and I was dying, the current tearing through my flesh like a shoal of piranhas swimming in my blood, and I screamed.

She must have switched it off because the pain was gone as suddenly as it had appeared, and she regarded me with an expression that said, quite clearly: *you're not getting out of here alive unless you satisfy my curiosity, which is considerable.*

"Chego angely bojatsja?" I said to her, and I saw her flinch. *What do angels fear?*

She blinked twice, and then she left me there and locked the door and I was left in the cell, breathing, relaxing the muscles, trying to get rid of the taste of bile in my mouth.

What do angels fear, I'd asked her, and I'd seen the question penetrate. It had been the wriggling worm at the end of the hook and she had taken it.

I waited. There was no sound in that place, and yet it seemed to me I could, if not hear, nevertheless *feel* the world around me, a dark, pervasive presence that infused the silent walls with an unnatural menace.

A darkness deeper than the absence of light detached itself from the wall and stood in front of me then. Dark eyes regarded me in silence.

His wing span was over two metres, the feathers obsidian black and as sharp as razorblades. The face was an indistinct darkness, a blur of still movement. He was full of paradoxes and even more of threat, and suddenly I thought, *I didn't bargain for this,* and then Azrael moved until his face was almost upon my own, his lips brushing mine, and he spoke in a whisper that ran down my spine like poisoned wine. "Angels fear nothing. Nothing. Nothing."

I felt his hand on my throat, a caress that turned into a strangle; his eyes threatened to draw me out of myself and be absorbed. His eyes burned like a multicoloured flower drenched in kerosene and set on fire. The air around us hummed, charged with electricity, and I could feel the walls moving in and out of my perception as if the prison itself was gasping for breath.

For the tortured there is a fine line, a knife edge, which is their breaking point. The secret is to live on the edge.

With Azrael, I stayed there for a long time.

It was less an interrogation than an expression of rage, and it made my resistance easier, hoarding away all the little dirty secrets of the trade in my mind, thinking of nothing, keeping the Bureau safe.

It's the only way to survive.

"What," I said, through teeth that were clenched around the little air I had, "are angels afraid of, Archangel? Chego angely bojatsja?"

He let me go then, and left me to gain control of my breath as he pondered me from a distance, a huge puddle of darkness in the room. His next words came slowly, oozing like rivulets of revulsion. "Have you come to kill me?"

He came near again and bent down, looking at me. His wings rustled and I could feel his breath, faintly sweet against my face.

"You have traces of angel on you." His voice had changed, as if he were performing an autopsy, speaking into a tape recorder. Dry. Emotionless. "And the scent of Paris on your body. Raphael and Metatron." He sounded as if he had almost resigned himself to my answer. "Have you come to kill me?"

"No," I said. "I haven't."

I thought he was going to speak to me then, perhaps to confide, perhaps only to resume his interrogation, but then somebody turned on the light and an awfully familiar voice said, echoing in the darkness, *But I have.*

NINE

I SAW HIM through the bars, but he wasn't looking my way; in fact, he wasn't looking anywhere but right ahead, and he was in a hurry.

There were no guards, only a small unmarked door that led outside, and he got into the driver's seat of a car that was parked there.

Eldershott, it appeared, enjoyed quite a few unusual freedoms as a prisoner of Lubyanka.

My money and papers were still in the guards' possession. It seemed that, when they'd dragged me in, they hadn't expected me to claim them back.

They were right, though for the wrong reason.

I only had to walk a short distance to get a cab, and he was almost out of sight by then, so I asked the driver to step on it and she did, not saying a thing.

"He owes me money," I said, which seemed to merely confirm her suspicions, so that she slowly nodded.

It was crunch time, bring him in before he gets away, but I was beginning to think Control weren't that interested in that, perhaps, as much as in where he would go next, since everywhere he was, it seemed, Archangels died.

Which went for me as well. It wasn't a thought I liked to contemplate.

He got out at Yaroslavski train station. I followed him to the cashier, the one that handled foreign visitors, and heard him get a ticket on train number four, for its entire journey, no stops, second class.

I bought a second class ticket to Ekaterinburg from the Russian counter, handing over the money in roubles. It would take me half of the way on the same train, and then...

"It's me."

No clicks on the phone, no little interruptions in the line, no static electricity in the background.

"Don't worry, it's safe." And, "Have you got him?"

"Yes."

"Have you made contact?"

"Not yet."

"Good. Where are you now?"

"Getting on a train that's going to Beijing."

That seemed to throw him back a bit, but he soon returned with, "What do you need?"

Good man.

I told him what I wanted and could almost hear Seago nodding on the other side of the line, and he said, "Carry a copy of *Pravda* when you go onto the platform and leave it somewhere visible. You will be approached at Ekaterinburg."

Click.

It was as hot on the train as it was cold outside; there was a samovar in the corner at the edge of the corridor, and a small wood fire burning underneath, heating up the water.

The cabin was empty, and I put down the small bag of necessities I'd bought at the station and sat down, incredibly weary, and closed my eyes, listening for the shrill cry of the engine and the rhythmic motion of the wheels as they began to move. Eldershott was in the same car, two cabins down; I waited until the train was in motion before walking past his cabin, and he was in, and there was nowhere to go; I intended to keep an eye on him, but right now I was simply too tired. I returned to my cabin, climbed up to the top bunk, stretched out, and slept.

My dreams were troubled, and took me back to Lubyanka, to the dark, small cell and the dark angel, Azrael, and that terrible voice saying, *but I have.*

I felt a soft hand caressing my neck, then moving down, and somehow I was freed of the shackles. I stood up and turned slowly, and faced Sophie Stockard.

Sophie Stockard: grey eyes like the calm before a storm, set like stones into a heart-shaped face devoid of all colour. Petite build, but muscular, which must have come from the dancing.

She was dressed in a simple shift, grey and featureless, and her arms were bare and as pale as her face.

"Where is my Johnny?" it was the dancer Sophie speaking, the one I had begun to suspect was hidden inside, but she was hushed by the other.

Azrael, she said, and there was a tone of amused malevolence in her voice. *How good to see you again.*

I looked at the angel, and that strange distortion of my sight began again, so that the cell seemed to stretch into a long, dark tube or corridor, Azrael standing at its end, unmoving and still.

Have you nothing to say for yourself? Sophie enquired with the same malevolent laughter. She began advancing down the corridor, and its walls pulsed and shifted as if they were somehow alive. *Nothing to justify to me, to explain, to plead?*

There was silence from the Archangel.

My poor, poor Azrael, said that terrible voice, as Sophie started to close the distance between she and the angel, her thin body seeming to grow as it moved further away.

Then the angel attacked.

Azrael's dark body suddenly bloomed, those great black wings opening to their full span, and he flew at Sophie like a desperate animal, hands outstretched for her neck.

She hit him, her small fist connecting with his face with the impact of a rock thrown from a catapult, slamming him back against the wall, but Azrael recovered, lifted a wing and *sliced*, and the tip of those shimmering feathers cut through Sophie's arm.

Droplets of bright red blood splattered the wall like tiny diamonds.

Sophie barked laughter and her arm came up, no longer bleeding, the cut disappearing as I watched, and she grabbed the angel's wing the way a child might the wing of a butterfly, with a detached interest, and dangled him up in the air. The great angel, suspended by a child's hand.

The featureless bottom of the corridor started to shimmer and a hole of pure light began to grow, widening under the angel's suspended form. His bright eyes looked down, then moved up and gazed straight into Sophie's grey ones.

"One for sorrow," said Sophie, the other Sophie, in a numb, uneven voice. "Two for joy."

And three for a girl, the inhuman voice added, and Sophie took the angel and *folded* him, like a piece of origami, compacting the angel into a neat, small black cube.

She looked back at me and she was smiling, and there was nothing innocent or angelic or wholesome about that smile, and her eyes were pools in which I found myself drowning.

Then she dropped Azrael into the opening in the floor and the dark angel fell like a crumpled sheet of paper drifting down until it touched the light and brightness flared, and the angel was gone and the darkness was gone, and Sophie turned slowly round and said, "Watch my Johnny for me," and the other voice laughed, inhuman and cold, and she disappeared.

"No!"

I opened my eyes to the dim lighting of the cabin, a wide Slavic face peering with concern at me over the bunk. The train moved quietly underneath me.

"Vy chuvstvuete horosho?"

"Thank you, I'm fine," I said, also in Russian, and she let me be.

I sat up, then climbed down from the bunk to sit at the bottom one by the window. It was snowing heavily outside, the snow turning the landscape ghostly and pale and silent, and I tried to bring my breathing under control.

"Chaj?"

She came back into the cabin and I realised I hadn't even noticed that she'd left, but she had a mug of steaming tea in her hand and so I said, "Spasibo," and accepted it from her.

It was dark and thick and sweet, and it was hot, boiling hot from the samovar in the corridor, and I sipped it gratefully, thinking, *This mission isn't going as well as could be hoped.*

The train's rhythmic motion and the heat of the tea were making me sleepy again; I finished the mug and gave it back to the woman, thanking her again, and climbed back up to the bunk and stretched.

When Sophie had disappeared, the door to the cell had been left open. When I'd gone out, cautiously, I'd found two guards asleep on the hard floor and, as I walked through the compound, I encountered more sleeping bodies. I checked each one, two fingers to test their pulse at the neck, but they were all alive and I wanted to get out of there fast, before they woke up.

I still had to find Eldershott. I didn't expect to run into him there.

But there he had been, untroubled, it seemed, by anything around him, and I had followed him to the station and now I was on the number four train, direct to Beijing, six nights with almost no stops through Siberia and Mongolia, and it was the height of bloody winter.

I worried about what would be waiting at the other end of the journey, but then I thought, *Well, hopefully there won't be any angels there, not where we're going,* and I fell asleep and, if I dreamt, I don't remember.

TEN

SEAGO HAD SAID Ekaterinburg, but they already had someone waiting down the line when the train pulled into Perm station at six-twenty in the evening, Moscow time, just under twenty-four hours since I'd left the Russian capital. Snow covered the platform like a sheet of ice and snowflakes rushed in the air and swirled in complex eddies. The grey building was lit, but poorly; there were only two hawkers on the platform, looking shrivelled and cold in oversized coats.

There were few travellers either coming or going. I joined the back of a group of passengers going out for a stroll on the platform and bought noodles and peanuts and salami and bread; I didn't want to show myself in the dining cart yet, my main aim right now was to disappear from view until we reached Ekaterinburg.

I didn't bother with the *Pravda*, I didn't want to make unnecessary contact, but I spotted him as soon as he showed up on the platform.

Unassuming. Ginger-haired, moustached Englishman— or possibly a Scot—mid to late forties. Probably an agricultural engineer doing low-level intelligence for MI6, now seconded to the Bureau for the sole purpose of greeting me on the platform.

He kept looking round, no doubt for the *Pravda*, and I packed up what I'd bought and hurried back onto the train, passing by Eldershott's cabin as I went. He was on the top bunk facing in the direction of travel, and he was reading a book. His cabin-mate was an elderly Mongolian who sat on the lower bunk and sneezed as he pinched snuff from a small bottle between forefinger and thumb and brought it up to his nose.

I went back to my cabin—the Russian woman sharing it with me had got off at one of the small, five-minute stops that were dotted in the snow like the sudden enclaves of naked wood, and I made sure no-one else would be coming in by bribing the babushka whose job it was to keep order in the car and fill up the samovar with water, as well as to keep its fire stoked. The Russian economy, I sometimes suspected, depended entirely on the elderly babushkas and their endless little jobs.

I closed the door and locked it, then opened the bag and took the meagre portions I'd purchased on the platform.

I hadn't eaten properly since Paris, and I was starving.

I didn't bother with the pleasantries. I tore a large chunk of bread (and say what you want, the Russians still make the best bread) and cut a large slab of salami and shoved both into my mouth.

I'd filled up the noodle pot with hot water on the way to the cabin, and now I waited for them to cook whilst eating more bread and salami.

I ate the noodles with my fingers, then drank the water like a soup. I felt better. I sat with the door closed as the train rocked away into the endless snow, enjoying the rare interlude this journey had offered. I ate the peanuts. Peanuts have all the nutrients the body needs. Their shells gathered around me like the remnants of used mortar left behind from a long-ago war.

I had been on the Trans-Siberian once before, fleeing a deadly agent of the KGB's Fourth Directorate, trying to stay alive and save the documents Conroy had managed to get from Star City before they'd found him. Now, I was beginning to feel inexorably lax, as if somehow the greater fear of the Archangels was enough to mute any feeling of immediate danger from their human subordinates. They called it the Great Game, and it was played only partially by humans, and I began to wonder who was playing against whom in this strange new war that was wiping out angels from both East and West.

But for now the game I had to play was patience, and I played it as well as I could as the train moved evenly onwards, through snow blizzards and the coming of the steppes, the landscape through the window looking like a giant white mirror, the air itself composed of slivers of sharp, deadly ice.

Once or twice I thought I saw figures moving in the eddies of snow, pale and beautiful beyond measure, with wings that beat evenly through the storm; but they moved in and out of my perception, an illusion of snowflakes blowing in the wind, and as I fell asleep, still propped against the table with peanut casings all round me, they came and haunted my dreams: angels, melting away like quicksand when I tried to grasp at their true shape, flying and swirling in the white silent storm.

ELEVEN

"WHAT HAPPENED?" THERE were people shouting around her, and I was already moving away, *Pravda* under my arm.

"She must have fallen, the poor dear," someone said in English, voice raised in the excitement of the moment. "Imagine it happening when we are on the Trans-Siberian Express, yes dear, that's right, the Trans-Siberian, this poor woman just fell from the train to the platform, and she almost died! I tell you, I was so frightened for her!" and I thought, *I hope she lives, but she won't be able to talk to anyone any time soon, or mention the Russian-speaking girl who paid her baksheesh on the train and disappeared in Ekaterinburg.* It was past midnight, six hours after we'd left Perm.

I bought another *Pravda* on the train and wasn't surprised to discover no mention of Azrael's death, or Metatron's either. It was obvious to me after being inside Lubyanka that the Russians were just as concerned as we were, and they were better at keeping unwelcome news quiet. Now I let the paper drop onto a bench, where it left a damp impression in the frost.

I walked away from the train, leaving the station, and felt rather than saw her following me under the arches.

I didn't have a lot of time and, though she was good, she was a local agent, not Bureau, just another agriculturalist or horticulturalist specialist or whatever it is they find to do in their official capacity in those two-horse Siberian towns.

"Have you got everything I asked for?"

Her accent was pure Oxford and colder than the snow. "Yes. Come with me."

She led me across the road into the foyer of a hotel. It looked abandoned. "You have less than half an hour," she said, "so we'd better hurry."

She took me upstairs to a small room—if there were staff at the hotel they were long-asleep at this hour—and brought out the equipment I'd asked for.

I spent the next twenty minutes altering my clothes and my hair, amazed as always by the transformation these small changes could make, but also aware that it wouldn't help deceive a trained operative.

Or an angel.

"I'll get rid of your things as soon as you're gone," she said.

I nodded. "Thanks."

She suddenly smiled. "No worries—it gets a bit boring down here. This is the most exciting thing I've had to do since the piping burst six months ago."

"Agriculture?"

"Irrigation. We're trying to build a model drip network for…oh, forget it."

I smiled. "Got long to go?"

"Six more months. Then somewhere hot, I hope. Africa, or the Middle East."

"Hope they fly by," I said. I picked up the bulky rucksack and adjusted the straps. "Be seeing you."

"Good luck."

She came with me, a few paces behind, back to the station and conferred with a short man standing in the shadows. He nodded twice and, without turning, she waved her hand in the air.

Eldershott was still on board. I couldn't acknowledge her—for one person to see me was enough, and her lookout made one too many—and I stepped onto the platform.

"Hello!" I called in English, and waved. I wore a smile like a new summer dress. "Wait!" and the new concierge, a tall, pale man with a thick dark moustache standing by the folding metal stairs leading into the cabin, looked at me in puzzlement, then waved me in when he saw my ticket.

I had the same cabin, as I'd specified to Seago back in Moscow. Marija Zita got on the train at Yaroslavski train station and got off at Ekaterinburg.

And Janet Gordon, English, twenty-eight, with a short blonde bob and comfortable, expensive hiking gear got on in her place. The only person who would have noticed was gone, and though I felt sorry for it, I knew it was necessary. She was gone and all anyone else had seen, if they'd seen anything at all, was Marija Zita.

I had the cabin to myself; the other three seats-cum-beds were reserved and wouldn't be claimed. I could trust Seago with that, at least. I spent an hour familiarising myself with the new identity before disposing of the dossier, keeping only the new identity documents. Then I headed to the dining cart.

He was sitting alone, at the furthest table in the corner of the cabin, eating Solyanka soup. The night outside was monochrome: white strips of land glaring in an inky dark. I took the only free table, sitting on the other side of the cabin from him and two tables down.

There were three Mongolians in heavy coats sitting by the door, smoking and drinking vodka and arguing. Next to them, a group of Western European tourists occupied three of the tables. I could hear German, Swedish and Dutch being spoken simultaneously, which would have been nauseating to follow, so I didn't.

Behind me sat a couple of male backpackers whose gazes I could feel against my back. I'd pegged them down as soon as I'd gone in. Blond, a big build, clean-shaven, they could have been hikers but they looked too clean, too comfortable in their surroundings, and I knew I was going to have to assess them again, and if they didn't check out, dispose of them.

"Da?"

"Oh, hi," I said, looking up at the waiter. My voice carried across the car and was noted. "Could I have a soup? I don't know the name for it, but I had a really lovely soup in Moscow before we left the station, do you know?" Looking at the pockmarked, stoic face hopefully: "Do you speak English?"

Eldershott hadn't risen to the bait, so I glanced back towards him, a hopeful expression on my face, then rose and went to him. "Excuse me, do you speak English?" I shook his shoulder, pointed down to his soup. To the waiter: "This is it!" Still pointing: "Could you bring me one of these please? How much is it?"

"*Odin* Solyanka." He noted it in his pad with a sort of grim determination and walked off.

There is a fine line you walk when you assume an identity. It has to be assumed completely, worn like a second skin, absorbed and displayed to the world without fault. The moment you slip, the moment you fall out of character, the moment suspicion falls is your last. The operation had shifted since Moscow, assumed a new shape and a new aspect, and I had shifted with it, going into second gear and putting a new play into motion, and I let Killarney fade into the core and let Janet Gordon, loud and charming and naïve, a master's degree in archaeology, never before left England, everything new and wonderful, take over. I needed access to Eldershott, and Janet was desperate for some English conversation to re-live her exciting new experiences.

"What did he say?" I asked Eldershott, still holding him by the shoulder. He looked over at me, eyes narrowed behind unflattering glasses. It was the first time I'd seen him close and face to face, and I committed him to memory, etching his face, his clothes, his build into my memory.

Eldershott: dark hair and thinning on top, with a bushy moustache that tried to compensate, unsuccessfully, for the high forehead and the weak chin, eyes pale blue and smoky like haze over the North Sea. His fingers were blunt but well-kept, and he had hair growing on his knuckles. He looked at me without expression for a long moment before sighing loudly and saying, "One Solyanka. Solyanka is the name of the soup."

"Thank you."

He shook my hand off his shoulder and returned to his bowl, lifting up a spoon in silent determination, turning his back on me. Hoping I would go away.

I wouldn't.

Check for weapons: none that I could see, and none on the two blond backpackers who were now obviously checking me whilst trying to look as though they weren't.

That changed things. I had to think quickly, trying to figure out where they came from. They could have been Russian, but I had a feeling that, whilst Eldershott's presence in Lubyanka was indeed thanks to the Fourth Directorate, him leaving it wasn't. We went straight from the prison to the station and got on the train, there was no time for anyone to mount an operation and yet here they were, like two concrete blocks cast in the same mould, two big blond twins, and I knew that sooner or later it would come to a standoff between us.

I still didn't know enough and I needed the information; I needed to understand Eldershott and who he was running from.

Or where he was running to.

"Are you English?" I tapped him on the shoulder again—Janet Gordon just trying to be friendly. "Do you mind if I sit with you? What's that that you're reading?" There was a rhythm to it, a kind of breathless excitement and a propensity for rapid-fire questions that didn't require immediate answers.

"I really don't think…" he began, but I was already in motion, sitting opposite him and waving to the waiter to signal my new location—as if he couldn't tell—all the time keeping up a monologue directed at Eldershott. "Can I see the book? What is it? Oh, it's old, isn't it! It's so lovely!" the last pronounced as two separate words, a long accent on *love* and a slightly shorter one on the suffix.

As I spoke I picked up the book and examined it, running a finger along the pages to see if anything was laid inside the pages, which there wasn't, and noting the title and the name of the author.

Military History since the Coming.

A picture, possibly authentic but more likely a photo-realist later impression, of Allied soldiers dropping their guns on the muddy ground before the Archangel Metatron, as he manifested before them.

"You're a historian?" My food finally arrived and I thanked the waiter with an awkward "Spasibo" that made Eldershott look at me again, suddenly.

"No," and, "Do you speak Russian?" The eyes narrowed again behind the glasses like clouds forming over a blue-grey sea.

"A little," I admitted. "My grandmother's maiden name was Kobach. She often spoke it to me. When I was younger. Do you?"

"What?"

"Speak Russian."

"I speak quite a few languages," he said, stating a fact or trying to impress me, it didn't matter; what did was that he had taken the bait now and was talking.

He had taken the bait and it was time to leave him to chew on it for a while, so I ignored him and concentrated on the food.

It came with a plate of the dark, sour bread only the Russians could make so well, and I scooped up a spoon of Solyanka—sausages, ham, onions, olives, there was little that didn't make it into this soup—and I soaked up the sour cream and lemon broth with the rest of the bread and washed it down with water, and when I was done, I signalled the waiter for another.

"Oh, and *dva peva!*" I called after him.

Eldershott was examining me again, his hand resting between two pages of the book; they were full of scribbles in the margins. I decided it might be handy for me to examine the book more thoroughly later.

"One is for you," I said, as the waiter brought over two large bottles of Baltika beer and deposited them on the table.

Again, I seemed to startle him. I couldn't read him; he seemed to be a mixture of meekness and aggression and he moved between the two almost without noticing. "Thank you, Miss…?" he trailed off, leaving me to fill him in.

"Gordon. Janet Gordon. Pleased to make your acquaintance," I said, formally, then smiled as he offered his hand. "As a thanks for helping me out," I said, pushing one of the beers towards him. "Mr…?"

"Morcombe," he said. "Thanks again."

"Well, Mr Morecombe, it's a pleasure to meet you."

Then the second bowl of soup arrived and I concentrated on that, ignoring him and yet observing his reactions, his signals. He wasn't tense but he was on some kind of edge, and that made him unpredictable; his fingers kept tracing invisible runes in the open book, and his eyes blinked like two flies trying to escape from solidifying amber.

The second bowl helped, and the beer was good. When I finished eating, I sat back against the window with my feet up on the seat.

"I'm an archaeologist," I said into his silence. "I'm going to work on a dig they have in the Gobi desert. Are you planning to stop in Ulaan-Bataar, too, or are you going on straight to Beijing?"

His ticket was all the way and so was mine, now, but I had a suspicion he wouldn't be going that far, and his reaction when I mentioned the Gobi was interesting, the eyes shifting to the window where the snow kept blowing in the icy wind. His fingers kept scribbling, faster and faster, on the pages of the book.

The Gobi, then?

Perhaps. But I didn't think so.

Either way, he didn't answer, and when he finally looked at me, his eyes were haunted, the orbs as large as moons in a pearly cloud, and he breathed once, deeply, and then his fingers stopped their motion and fell silent and he slumped in his seat, his head almost hitting the table and blood coming out of his mouth.

TWELVE

THEY WERE WAITING for me in the space between the cabins, a narrow metal enclosure with a window on one side and a door on the other and the smell of stale cigarettes permeating it.

The first one tried to grab my arm and I twisted, my knee finding the soft place between his legs, and he grunted but didn't let go. I felt the second one move and I kicked out, a backward kick that connected and threw him against the window. The first one landed a punch in my ribs, hard, and I nearly collapsed from the pain, and then he released me and I stood, gasping for air between the two of them as both slowly straightened up and looked at me.

Blond, bulky, and dangerous. It was too late at night, nobody could hear us, nobody would wander past or go for a late cigarette.

The one by the door kicked out then, a high kick that would have connected with my neck had I not blocked it, and I ducked under and punched him in the stomach in a one-two-one rapid movement but his arm came up and hit me on the side of the face, and then the second one was there, trying to grab me from behind in a Nelson lock, and I went mad. There are no rules to krav maga, only to inflict as much damage on your opponent as quickly as you can, but these weren't amateurs; they were good, so I let Anna Gordon dissipate and Killarney take over, the organism cornered and frightened and angry, and my foot flew back between his legs and connected, and he let me go, briefly.

It was enough, and I turned round and ducked as the first one aimed another punch at my face that almost connected with his friend's. I tried to trip him, hooking my foot into his and using his own body weight against him and it worked, throwing him against the door, but his friend was already up and on me—and I knew I couldn't go on for very long with these two, they were pros and they were big—and he grabbed me in a bear hug, and I twisted, kicking in the air as he held my body, and somehow managed to press the lock on the door and throw it open.

Freezing air came rushing into the cabin and I could see the tracks running past and the beginning of light in the distant horizon.

I kicked out again and by luck it connected, hitting the first one in the chest and pushing him against the wall and closer to the open door.

The one who was holding me tightened his grip and I felt my arm fracturing, that sick sound of bones being slowly broken, and in desperation I used him as my springboard, feeling a bone breaking as I did but I lashed out with both legs and *pushed*, and my feet connected with the man by the door and threw him outside, where his short scream disappeared behind the moving train.

I was on more even ground now and he knew it, but he had the advantage and now I'd pissed him off, and I could hear another bone going and thought, *No, this isn't how it ends,* and I twisted, releasing myself somehow and hitting him with an open hand on the neck before landing my thumb in his windpipe.

He hit me on the side of the head, hard, but I just kept pushing and his breath turned to a choke, and I dropped him to the ground and landed my elbow in his neck, over and over, until he stopped moving.

It was hard to breathe but it wasn't over, and so I rolled him on the floor, wincing in pain and as I did his hand turned and I saw the tattoo on his wrist, a red, inverted swastika and the wings on each side; the same as the dead girl I'd left in a Parisian loo, and I thought, Damn, *who the hell* are *these people,* and then he was by the door and dangling out, and I pushed him, but he wouldn't move and I had to kick his head, and the fourth or fifth time finally did it and he dropped.

I cursed them for not giving me the chance to find out who they were, and cursed again as I catalogued the damage they had caused. Split lip, what felt like broken bones in my left arm, and the skin on my face felt raw and bloodied. I've had worst but this was bad timing, and I knew that I couldn't stay on the train all the way to Beijing now, and I still wasn't sure what to do about Eldershott.

In the dining cart, he'd almost fallen into his food, and I'd done the only thing I could think of, lying him on the ground and trying to make him breathe, and when he did I shoved my fingers into his mouth and made him puke, his food coming out purple and red, with mucus and blood intermingled.

He could have been poisoned, but when he regained consciousness he shoved me away as if nothing had happened and walked out of the dining cart with an awkward step, and I still couldn't read him, couldn't read him at all. Something had happened to him on the train, something had reached over and he'd almost died, and I didn't know why.

Eldershott. He was alive, but he had almost made me break my cover and all the explanations about how Janet Gordon once took a first-aid course weren't going to amount to much; we had both become focal points of interest and I didn't want that. I needed to operate in the dark and this was far too visible.

And then there were the blond twins, and that strange tattoo again, and the door flopping open in the cold Siberian wind as the train snaked away into the distance. Someone had left a packet of cigarettes lying on the floor, Prima, and there was one cigarette still in it, a little crushed but it would do, and I lit it, thinking the hell with abstinence, blond killers or angels or both.

The nicotine spread through my bloodstream and into my head, making me light-headed. I thought back to Paris and to the girl in the bathroom, the one I'd had to kill, and to that nameless Irish bartender and the equally-nameless sniper who'd killed him.

I'd assumed the opposition were Russians to begin with, but I didn't think that was the case anymore—the Russians would be just as worried as the Bureau—so there must be bsomeone else operating on this mission, running a counter-action to the one I was running. I needed to find out who they were and what was going on, and I decided it was time to stop pussy-footing around; I didn't have much time left and the train was becoming dangerous, and Eldershott would have to talk, one way or the other.

But first I needed to take care of myself. The train was moving, and Eldershott would be safe in his cabin for a while longer—at least I hoped he would. I shut the door on the night and the snow outside and went to my cabin. They had searched it thoroughly, and I went through everything carefully, checking for traps, but they'd obviously thought they could finish me off by themselves and hadn't bothered.

They'd been wrong not to bother, but it was too late to tell them that. I bandaged my arm and cleaned my face and climbed up onto the top bunk and fell immediately asleep.

THIRTEEN

I HAD TO hurry at Omsk station because the train wouldn't be stopping for very long, and I almost waved the copy of *Pravda* in the air before dropping it. I stuck to protocol, but it cost me.

The local agent was a short, skinny lad with nervous brown eyes, and I thought, *They're really scratching the bottom of the barrel here,* though I could be wrong; you don't get sent to Siberia unless you can handle it, and there aren't that many agents who can.

"I need to see Seago," I said. "Straight away."

He blinked, and I said, "Did you get that?" my voice rough, and he blinked again and nodded without speaking. The next stop was Barabinsk but it wouldn't do; it wouldn't give Seago time to get there, so it had to be Novosibirsk and I had a bad feeling about that.

I had a bad feeling about the entire thing, and I was getting worried about Eldershott. He hadn't come to the dining cart the next day, and when I'd looked into his cabin he was spewing black blood again, but when I tried to check him over his eyes opened and he pushed me away, not speaking, and wiped his mouth with a handkerchief as if nothing had happened. The handkerchief was stained with old blood.

He looked up at me. "What do you want?" he demanded, then saw my face and stopped still. "What happened to you?"

"I cut myself shaving."

He didn't know how to take that, and I looked at the dark blood on his handkerchief, and he followed my gaze and back. "Look, don't come in here again, all right? I suffer from fatigue, and sometimes I black out." He could see I didn't believe him. He was like a dying man saying he'd never felt better.

"It's nothing serious."

I nodded, slowly, and it was evident something had shifted in our interaction, that he was wary of me, and that wasn't good either, because he had no way of knowing who I was unless the opposition agents weren't there to trail him, they were there to guard him and, if that was the case, he must have been unpleasantly surprised to see me in his cabin.

I waited outside until he left the cabin and locked the door behind him and went to the bathrooms, and then I picked the lock. I had to be quick, but I went through his stuff methodically, searching under the mattresses, behind the loudspeakers that woke us each morning with shrill Russian programmes, finally through the small, dark leather bag that seemed to be his only possession.

Inventory: three pens, two black and one blue; three pairs of underwear, Woolworths; two shirts, Marks and Spencer; four pairs of socks from same, dark green; one book, *Military History Since the Coming*, the same one he'd had with him in the dining car. I went through the pages more thoroughly than I had been able to before, but there was still nothing hidden inside it.

Nothing else in the bag, nothing in his coat pockets either—and was that a commotion outside, had he tried to open the door and couldn't? I listened carefully but it was nothing, only my imagination playing up, and I knew I had to hurry.

No notes, no writing, nothing to indicate what he was doing here in the middle of Nowhere, Siberia, in the depths of winter.

I'd checked for the little traps we always leave on our stuff when we're in the field—the hair on the spine of a book, the clothes lined up at a specific angle, all the little things we do to see if anyone has been there, but there was none. Elder- shott was clean; he wasn't a pro, or else he was so good that I couldn't detect it.

I didn't think he was that good. Whatever he was, he wasn't a field agent.

I made sure everything was left exactly as I'd found it.

Except for the book.

There was nothing to indicate it was anything but a nor- mal book but there was something about it, maybe the way Eldershott tapped his fingers on it the whole time he sat in the dining car; he behaved as if the book was a lifeline and when they do that, it's usually because it is; it has some special significance for them. I thought it was a lifeline and I decided to cut it for him. I wanted him on the defensive; I wanted him nervous now, and I wanted to run him, not be run blindly myself.

I was back in my cabin when he finally got out of the bath- room and, afterwards, he was silent, and I began to read the book carefully, still searching for the hidden codes but I hadn't found them and I was getting edgy because I knew something had to be there.

Omsk, the train silent by the platform, the railway stretching into white fog like a gate into another world.

"Get in touch with Seago," I said again, wondering where they'd got an agent from in Omsk, "and tell him to be there at Novosibirsk when the train arrives. Tell him to meet me on the platform. Do you understand? And to be ready to activate whatever pisspot network we have operating down there."

He nodded again, and I was getting irritated. It was important he got it right, and I made him repeat it before getting back on the train. There were still eight hours to Novosibirsk, and so I sat back in the cabin and opened Eldershott's little book and read, for the umpteenth time, the history of the world since the Coming of the Angels, back at the end of the Second World War.

It was an old story: how the angels began to materialise above the battlefields and death camps of Europe, appearing wherever blood was spilt and mass death occurred. I flicked through the illustrations again: Azrael manifesting in the gas chambers of Auschwitz, Raphael appearing in Normandy, Behemoth—the largest of all the Archangels, who now resided in St. Paul's—come into being in the midst of the Germans' aerial bombardment of London.

It was the same old shit: the end of the war, and the Coming of the Angels. They settled where they wished, and in the intervening years they played their curious games: Raphael and his drug cartel, connections and gambling; Azrael in Lubyanka, turning the prison into a miniature hell on earth;

Metatron sprawling with all his massive bulk inside Notre Dame, where fools came to worship him.

Now all three were dead and I had to find out why.

I had nearly finished reading when the window exploded and a hot searing pain cut through my hand and fragments of broken glass hit my body like tiny razorblades, and through foggy eyes I saw in very slow motion, my blood dripping onto the pages of the book, each drop suspended for a moment in the air, a frozen red ruby, and then everything sped up again and I rushed headlong into a cold ocean of darkness.

FOURTEEN

THE SKY WAS the colour of freshly-washed linen and, between the low-lying clouds, angel wings beat a measured tempo.

I stood on a ground as white as the skies, a featureless expanse of paleness devoid of any signs of life. It was a clean place, an empty place, a sterile place, and my blood fell on the ground like the red petals of a flower and stained it like a wound.

I stood and watched angels fly on the high winds.

Angels: wings that stretched six or seven metres from tip to tip, razor-sharp white feathers cutting through the cold, clean air like heated knives. Angels: strangely human heads that swivelled this way and that, with eyes that were fathomless pools of mixed grey and milky whiteness, eyes that I could feel examine me from high up, from the cold clear winds of those enormous skies. Angels: circling on the wind like giant birds, swooping low and coming back up again, majestic and care-free and dangerous birds of prey.

I felt strangely devoid of urgency, as if I had stumbled into a dream world in which dream logic applied, where my wounds were only a detail of the dream; when I looked down, the bleeding had stopped and my injuries seemed to have suddenly disappeared.

I sat down on the ground and pulled my feet up under me, and watched the angels fly in the vast, featureless sky.

I remembered the window breaking, the pain in my hand. Someone must have been shooting at the train, shooting at the window, shooting at me.

And I must have been shot, and this was the result: that I was now hallucinating, that I was dreaming this place.

And yet I could feel the cold. That was real enough, the sort of cold that penetrates into the bone, that makes you want to claw your face to draw warm blood, anything to warm up. It felt very real, that aspect of it. It had the kind of coldness that shakes you awake.

And it had an alien essence about it, a strangeness and a wrongness that said I did not belong there, that this was not my world.

The shadows of the angels flittered on the ground like giant, shifting shapes. As I watched, the shadows congealed and came together into one massive blotting of light, and as I sat and waited, a shape slowly appeared, titanic and yet indistinct, descending from the skies to land before me.

A giant head regarded me from a height. Eyes the size of lakes set in a craggy face, a face like a weathered mountainside where little grew or lived or breathed.

A vast mouth opened, and a sound like a hurricane emanated from it.

It was one word.

Just one word.

It was a name.

Killarney, the voice said.

"What are you?" I said, but even as I spoke, my voice dissipating in the cold, clean air, I knew the answer to my question.

As above, so below.

"I don't understand."

You will, Killarney, the giant mouth said, and in its voice was the sound of leaves in autumn and the coming of snow. And: *Too long have the Fallen escaped me.*

"What shall I do?" I felt lost and small, a child amongst giants, seeking answers to questions I didn't even know to ask.

The man you follow is both more and less than a man. The cipher and the key.

The giant moved like an avalanche, and its breath carried down to me and brought with it images: snow and ice and loneliness, and in the whiteness of the desert of ice, a building, human-made and impregnable.

"I don't understand," I said again.

You will, it promised again. *When the time comes, you must destroy the key.*

I was being given nonsensical answers in a dream, and the reality of the place seemed diminished as if it were beginning to fade.

You will shortly wake up, back in your world. Remember this dream. When the time comes, you will know what to do.

Its shape began to shimmer like ice melting. Its last words were a lost whisper catching at the edge of consciousness. *Fair well, Killarney. We shall meet again, before this is over.*

My eyes snapped open.

Pain, my hand throbbing, multiple cuts on my upper body adding to my previous injuries. Broken bones, a cut-up face.

At this rate I'll be dead before the next train stop, I thought, then realised the lull of the moving train was gone, that I was on solid ground, and that the face looking down at me without expression was human, not angelic.

It was Seago.

"What the hell is going on?" I tried to say, but my mouth didn't work and I was drifting again, my eyes closing, seeing only white, icy and cold and, in the distance, the aerial dance of angels…

FIFTEEN

"YOU ARE A brave woman."

He had a Russian accent, but the words were English and clearly pronounced. He sat by my bed with a mug of steaming tea in his left hand. His right arm was missing.

By the window, Seago shot him a warning glance. "No."

"No what?" I said, my lips dry and my mouth tasting as if frogs had been mating inside it.

Seago ignored me. "Enough. I'm taking her out. We'll send in someone else. Thornton and Kurt are waiting in Beijing."

"No." the Russian drank noisily from his mug, and I was getting pissed off at being ignored like this. "She is important. Like it or not, but she is linked to the nodus. It was she who killed Raphael, and how many people do you know who've killed an angel and are still alive?"

"She is not capable of continuing the mission." Seago's mouth was a thinly-drawn line in an angry face. He looked fatigued, and his voice was rough with cigarette smoke.

I tried to sit up and succeeded, though my vision clouded for a minute and I had to breathe hard before it abated.

At least I had their attention now.

"Where," I said carefully, "am I?"

The Russian and Seago again exchanged glances.

"Welcome to Novosibirsk," the Russian said finally. "I hope your journey was as pleasant as could be desired?"

I didn't appreciate the attempt at a joke. "And who the hell are you?"

But memory came flooding back even as he spoke, and I remembered the arm that was no longer there, and knew where it had been lost.

"Colonel Sergei Abramovich, Komitet Gosudarstvennoi Bezopasnosti at your service."

Abramovich. KGB. The man they called The Hunter. His pursuit of escaped Nazis was legendary, as was their eventual fate. Abramovich was of the shoot first, ask later school of spying. The highest ranking Jew in the Directorate, he'd lost his arm capturing Eichmann in the jungles of Borneo in '59.

"I thought you were dead."

"No, just busy."

He must have been over seventy, though you couldn't tell that by looking at him.

They were both looking at me now, and I had to think fast because this changed the picture and I didn't understand it. I was shot and I should have been in police custody now, if not KGB, and I wasn't, at least not quite. I had Seago for local Control and he seemed comfortable enough in Abramovich's presence, and that worried me because we're not exactly buddies with the Russians and this had to be serious if they were somehow cooperating. So, instead of asking questions, I swung myself out of bed and stood up, shaking, and went to the bathroom where I was sick.

I had a quick shower and put on clothes that were waiting for me there, and when I got out I felt better, and I helped myself to a mug of tea from the samovar in the room.

"Brief me."

They exchanged that look again but then Abramovich nodded and Seago said carefully, "Someone assassinated Behemoth at St. Paul's and the Prime Minister is highly strung—"

I looked at him and he looked back, and he said, "He's threatening to push the button, and the Russians are doing the same."

I nodded. I said, "How?" meaning Behemoth, and he understood that and said, "We don't know. There was a five-minute memory blackout in a mile-wide radius around the cathedral and now there's no Behemoth and no St. Paul's either."

I closed my eyes, and an image came into my head, unbidden: Sophie Stockard—in that loose hospital nightgown and bare feet, and that inhuman voice coming out of that human mouth—walking up to the cathedral. Somehow, though, I didn't understand how; I could see her, unhurried, calm, the grey eyes cold, bare feet over bare stone and the voice saying *ashes to ashes, dust to dust*, as Behemoth was reduced to nothing and was gone.

"Killarney? Killarney!"

Seago was shaking me, and I snapped up and said, "I know who did this," but it didn't seem to register, and they exchanged that look again, and I knew they were still arguing about me and I was going to have to put a stop to it there and then.

"I'm fine," I said. "And I'm going to finish this." I let that sink in, then added, "Now explain to me what the KGB is doing here, and in God's name tell me you didn't lose Eldershott."

"Not the KGB, *per se*," Abramovich said with a slight apologetic air, "I'm afraid my comrades in the service are less willing to consider all the relevant factors than I am. I was able to pull enough muscle to get you off that train and get you here, but I'm afraid once you leave this room, you're on your own."

"Eldershott got off at Novosibirsk," Seago added. He was looking out of the window again as if searching for something in the pale greyness outside, something he'd lost long ago and still couldn't find. "He wasn't going to Beijing, Killarney. He was coming straight here, and he was picked up at the station by some old friends of Colonel Abramovich."

A look of pure, unrestrained hatred flashed over Abramovich's face for the briefest part of a second before his tight smile returned. But the hate remained in his eyes. I didn't think it would ever leave them. "I regret to say my government was more tolerant of the Nazis than I first thought. At least, *some* Nazis. As it's turned out, they brought quite a few of them back after the war."

"So did the Americans," Seago pointed out.

I remembered that. I said, "Scientists?"

Seago nodded. "Mainly. It seems friend Eldershott is quite chummy with them."

"I don't understand."

Seago turned from the window. Whatever he was looking for out there, he still couldn't find it. He had the look of a man who knew he never would. "I'm not sure we do, either. Eldershott was clean."

I waited him out.

"We had him vetted," he said. "At intervals. Standard procedure. He was clean."

"Until Paris, then," I said.

"Yes." He sighed. "The most likely explanation is that they somehow turned him when he was in Paris, but we still don't know why he's important to them. He was just a cryptographer."

"Working on angel-related problems?"

A shrug, conceding the point. The KGB man didn't let go of his smile. Seago said, "Abramovich couldn't find out quite what is going on. All we know is that there is a research facility that doesn't officially exist, about a hundred and fifty miles out of Novosibirsk, and that Eldershott was taken there from the train."

In *the whiteness of the desert of ice, a building...* I shook my head, trying to dispel the sudden dizziness. When I opened my eyes, Seago and Abramovich seemed to have reached a sort of agreement between them.

Abramovich coughed, said "You need to, of course, recuperate from your injuries." His one remaining hand was stroking a white beard and, apologetically, he said, as Seago nodded like an albatross by the window, "But we'd like you to penetrate that facility. At your earliest convenience, please."

SIXTEEN

THE SOUND OF the engine filled the night like the buzz of a rusting chainsaw, and we were speeding along the tarmac and into the dark skies above.

There was no moon, and I sat back inside the Cessna whilst the pilot took us into the air, flying low over the frozen landscape. No moon, only the distant glow of thousands of stars, duplicated below in the ice in a ghostly reflection.

It took me six days to heal enough for me to be willing to do it. Six long days—and not nearly enough time for the bones to heal or the cuts to fade, but it was enough, and throughout those six days, Seago and Abramovich paced and worried, and Eldershott was invisible, hiding somewhere inside that place in the ice, the place that wasn't officially there.

On the seventh day I was ready.

Over that period there had been two more angel killings, the one in Rome and the other in Haifa, a port city in the south of Israel. There were only ever a few angels in America but, had one been assassinated, the Americans would have had to get involved, and the threat of a nuclear war would have become almost inevitable. But it was hard to find angels in America, thankfully.

Six long days: Seago smoked too many cigarettes; Abramov-ich drank too many cups of tea. I waited. Six days didn't seem like a long time if I thought of what waited at the end of them.

I tried not to, practiced killing in an empty room instead.

Meanwhile, nothing had been seen of Eldershott, and no word had come through any of the networks as to the pur-pose of the research facility. There was a big cloud of silence over that installation in the ice, a chasm where none should have been.

I was going to fall into that chasm. A part of me chafed at being inactive. I could grow bored very quickly trying to kill the air. The mission was entering its last, and most dangerous, stage, and I was ready to go, I was ready to finish it.

There was no word from any of the Archangels; they had kept silent about the killings as if trying to deny they had ever happened. The situation was getting tense, and the pressure was affecting Seago, who spent hours communicating on the radio with London every night, receiving information, giving none back, dead ash

collecting at his feet like a grey Whitehall carpet. All Lon-don knew was that the mission was still active—the Bureau may have been compromised and Seago wasn't about to let them compromise the mission, what was left of it.

What was left of it was me.

We flew blind, on instruments and a certain amount of hope. It was a hundred and fifty miles to the target, but get-ting too close would be suicide and I would have to hike the last twenty-five alone.

This is what Abramovich had gathered: the facility employed a large number of ex-Nazi scientists, most of them brought back after the war but some—so Abramovich said in a voice as devoid of emotion as a hastily-erected tombstone—were apparently brought later by ODESSA, the Nazi network that saw so many wanted men slip away from the Allies and disappear, after the war.

"ODESSA," he had said. Were their agents the ones who had attacked me, the ones attempting to stop anyone on Eldershott's trail? We didn't know. Had the Nazis infiltrated the Fourth Directorate of the KGB? The Kremlin? Or were the old scientists being used by someone else for purposes we didn't know and couldn't understand?

We didn't know. All Seago and Abramovich knew, joining forces reluctantly, was that they couldn't trust anyone else, not in Moscow, and not in London either.

It left them no-one but me. There was no-one else to send, not here, not now. It came down, simply, to me finishing the mission.

Which suited me fine. I always work alone.

The pilot shouted through the roar of the engine and signalled down with his thumb. I acknowledged it, released the seatbelt and forced the door open.

Wind blasted into the small aeroplane, bringing with it frost and the promise of worse to come. The temperature plummeted. I held onto the frame and pushed myself against the wind until it came at me like a fist and punched me loose, away from the plane and into the black and white Siberian night.

I fell, and as I did, the parachute opened and I breathed a sigh because I don't like parachuting. I do it only when I really have to; they're too easy to sabotage and I should know—I removed two senior members of the Romanian Securitate that way once.

It's not a nice way to go.

I dropped heavily onto solid ice and rolled with difficulty, my body flaming in pain once again. It would stop me if it could, but I wasn't going to let it. Instead, I collected the parachute and hid it under a pile of snow. Then I began to walk.

I was still about twenty-five miles from the target, and I had to get there fast. I unfolded the telescopic skis and attached them to my boots and then I took out the goggles Seago had given me, starlight vision, and I attached them and turned them on and twilight suddenly grew over the horizon.

It is a strange sensation, skiing in complete silence through a landscape that has nothing of the human in it. The goggles gave everything a pale aura and bathed the icy world with pale shadows. It was hypnotic, gliding on ice with nothing but the stars for company, and it made me think again of the dream I'd had, of that pale, sterile world of ice in which a giant being spoke to me in riddles...

Perhaps I had been going on for too long. I didn't know. I began seeing new shapes in the artificial shadows, vast and sharp like the outlines of wings, and grey chasms like Sophie's eyes, at once human and alien. There were white lights glowing behind the shadows, like milky pale eyes, watching me from their hiding places: ice and snow, the frozen siblings.

My speed escalated, and I felt as if I were being pushed by a giant hand across the fields of ice, gathering momentum.

It was strange and exhilarating, that silent race in the starlight, and I flew ahead, flying as if I, too, had wings, as if I, too, were—for just one tiny moment—an angel.

Then, like a fist coming out of the sky, the ice exploded around me and I was thrown, hard, landing awkwardly in a pile of hard snow.

Numbly, I stared up at the sky. I didn't know what had happened. Something had thrown me, but as to what it had been I could see no sign. All was quiet, and peaceful, and cold. Somewhere high above, movement like the passing of giant wings…

I didn't know what had happened, but it had saved my life. I sensed rather than saw the movement in the distance. Coming closer.

They were too far away yet, and too well-trained, to betray themselves by sound. White shadows moving against white snow…and had I continued skiing, my trajectory would have delivered me straight into their laps.

Which was something I was quite eager to avoid.

Instead, I stood up, removed the skis and folded them away, and circled cautiously round them, giving the approaching party a wide berth. I saw them from a distance, crouching behind a boulder, the goggles—somehow still on my head, still working—showing them to me in starlight.

There was nothing distinct about them, just a group of soldiers wrapped up heavily, with guns slung over their shoulders. They didn't look tense, and I left them to it and walked on until, suddenly, I crested a small hill and found myself staring at the frozen monstrosity that was the research facility, and I thought, *This is going to be a hell of a lot more difficult than I thought.*

SEVENTEEN

HE MOVED TOO slowly and besides, I came at him from behind; he didn't have a chance, and I cut his throat with a knife and caught him in my arms as he fell, dropping him gently to the ground.

Red mixed with white and I had a flash of memory, the red swastika tattoo and the wings on each side, promising death.

The research facility was a fortress carved in the ice. Icy turrets and frozen walkways and, behind the walls, the sense of an invisible presence. The beams of powerful searchlights criss-crossed the ice just beyond.

I had come on it almost by accident as if it had sprung, magic-castle-like, out of the ice where, a moment before, nothing had been. There were no fences, no battlements; they wouldn't have been necessary. There was only the castle, solid ice and impregnable to sight, squatting like a malevolent angel sculpted in snow and shadows; what lay behind its walls I could only guess at.

The place had an eerie silence about it, an absence of sound that didn't seem natural even in the midst of this quietude of ice. Consulting my wristwatch—I thought it might have stopped at some point during my rush across the ice, but no, the entire journey had taken me less than half the time I had thought it would.

I worried that my speed, too, wasn't entirely natural.

I circled the facility from a safe distance, trying to assess its security.

Watchtowers, four, one on each corner; searchlights; what looked like identical sets of machine-gun arrays below each tower. Soldiers, indistinct shapes, moving in the dark. There were no obvious openings, but I could see, at the bottom of one tower, slight humps in the ice that suggested hidden guard outposts.

As I circled, the pattern repeated; what entry there was into the castle was likely underground.

I needed to somehow reach those guard posts without being detected, and then, somehow, force my way inside, find Eldershott, abort whatever operation it was the Germans were running there, in the middle of the Siberian desert of ice. There were too many somehows in the equation, too many random elements I couldn't control, and I knew I would simply have to risk it, rely on the organism to keep me alive, to keep me going until I could finish the mission, and hope it would be enough.

It was cold, the ice penetrating through my suit with its dead, cold bony fingers, and I knew I would have to move fast, that staying out here for too long was in itself a death.

And so I did: I moved fast, crawling on the ice towards the castle's walls. My suit blended in with the colour of the snow, as I crawled towards the edifice. I hugged snow and crawled and tried not to think of the pain.

It was only a short distance, really, but when you're on your belly it's different, crawling and knowing those searchlights could find you in a careless second, and that you wouldn't even know it when they did. The sniper's bullets would make sure of that.

I didn't dare stop; I had to keep going until I reached the relative safety of the walls. When I approached close enough for me to hear voices, what I heard wasn't good—the guards spoke German, not Russian—and that most likely meant the Russians had lost control of their own facility. I wondered if they knew it. I wondered if the remains of the Russian guards were buried somewhere in the snow, white bones resting in a sea of white ice. I wondered who was running the facility now, and for what purpose. I wondered what I was doing there, but then let that one go.

The first of them didn't even notice when I cut his throat, he just died, quietly and politely and without making a fuss, but the second turned, gun at the ready and about to shout and raise the alarm, and I threw the knife at him, the blade still wet with his partner's blood, and the knife missed his heart but got the hand holding the gun and he dropped it, and before he could shout for help, I was there with a swivel kick to the head, and a follow up as he fell. I'd been aiming for the throat and, in a moment, he didn't have enough of a windpipe left to breathe with.

The entrance to their post was hidden in the ice; it was a round hole, wide enough, with an iron ladder leading down. I pulled their bodies, one by one, and lay them against the wall and tried to cover them with snow; just enough to make it difficult to detect if you weren't specifically looking for them. Then I climbed down the ladder.

The atmosphere grew warmer as I went down, a hidden air-conditioning unit humming in the background, and when

I reached the floor, I took off my gloves and my hat and pock-eted the goggles.

It was quiet down there, a featureless corridor of ice leading away towards the facility, and not a person in sight. I guessed they didn't figure on the need for much security past that point, but it still had me worried. They didn't need the kind of security they had, not out here, not even for a nuclear facility, but they still had it.

I came to a three-way intersection and chose the middle path, continuing straight ahead, trying to feel for any gradual changes in the level of the corridor, but it wasn't sloping or climbing. It was a level passageway, and there were no doors or windows, and no guards. I began to worry that this, too, was some kind of a trap, a maze of corridors leading nowhere, but then the level of the floor did change and I began moving downwards, deeper into the earth and, as I did, my perception began to change, and I could feel the strangeness I had felt before. It was slowly working its way into my mind.

In my double vision, the corridors assumed an eerie, ghostly second layer; hazy lines wavered almost beyond sight, resem-bling the anatomical representation of amputated angels' wings. My heart was beating faster, pushing the blood around the body as if trying to pump it away, and I tried to calm it but it was no use; it was as if I were being administered adren-aline externally and it was now making its presence felt.

I descended gradually, and as I did the lights became brighter and the corridor expanded, and then it stopped at a small, white door that said, simply, LABORBEREICH, *Lab-oratory Area*, and I opened it, and then the screaming started.

EIGHTEEN

THE CAGES WERE made of a strange, transparent material. They were arranged neatly around the room like kitchen utensils.

Inside the cages lay angels—or what remained of them.

The room was filled with cages occupied by angels. Torn wings, bodies convoluted in impossible ways, bloodied scars that ran from a few centimetres to the length of an entire body. Incisions, excisions, mutilations. The angels stared at me through bars, from faces beaten and empty, and their eyes were uncomprehending.

They screamed.

It was as if my presence alone was responsible for such fear in them, such agony that they could not unleash it in any other way. Their screams were terrible skull-piercing protestations of anger, fear and hate; they were both inhuman and awesome, grotesque and horrifying. The sound of their agony made me ill.

I nearly retched, their sound a violent, soul-tearing, penetrating knife, scoring blindly. There was no escaping that sound. I would have retched and stained that spotlessly clean floor if I hadn't spotted a pair of ear mufflers and reached for them, desperate, and put them on. They had been hanging on a hook above the door.

As soon as I put them on the sound ebbed. The angels continued to scream, but the tonal pain was being filtered out. I took a deep breath. It was a clean, well-lit place full of mutilated angels.

It was difficult to tear myself away from the sight; the once-majestic creatures, so arrogant in their dominance of our world, now crouched like beaten animals behind icy glass cages. And yet, as I examined them, I began to understand that there was something different about them, something different from the angels I had encountered before.

Perhaps it was simply the fact they were not, like Behemoth or Metatron had been, gigantic and obese. They were human-sized or smaller, but then so had Raphael been, so had the dark angel in Lubyanka.

Their feathers looked dishevelled and worn, and the wing-tips less sharp somehow, less of a deadly weapon. Their faces looked less human than I thought they should, the inherent alien nature of them more pronounced. I had a strange feeling these angels were unknown, that their names did not appear in any of the lists, but the idea was preposterous; the Coming began and ended after the Second World War, and no new angels had manifested since then, anywhere.

Or so I'd thought.

Cages, benches, and as I went through a door in the wall, an operating theatre. The table was crusted with blood and less easily identifiable body liquids, some congealed into a sort of grey scum. There were various instruments on display, screens currently turned off, an array of surgical implements, a sink with more blood stains on it, and the massive table in the middle like a slab of ice that looked as if whatever patients were brought to lie on it did not get the chance to rise from it again.

It made me feel sick, and I remembered where I had seen things like this before: the German death camps in Poland where the Nazis had experimented on countless victims in the name of science. That's what they looked like: the German laboratories.

There was a second door at the other end of the room and I opened it, glad to discover it led into another corridor, not another butcher's shop. I needed to locate Eldershott, and I needed to know what was being done in this place, or rather, to what purpose it was being done.

Fact: the entire facility was likely German. It looked as if the Russians had bitten off more than they could chew when they brought back Nazi scientists to work for them. That the Americans, the Brits and even the Egyptians had done the same was not a welcome thought.

Fact: they were conducting experiments on angels. On *angels*. While angels could be killed—for example, human blood caused them damage, at least if delivered in the right way—and there were stories of internal killings, when angels fighting for the same territory might dispose of each other. No-one knew how angels died, or why they died at all. They never discussed much—not where they came from, not God, nor what their ultimate goal was, or even if they had one.

Fact: someone was killing angels around the world. *Arch*angels.

Fact: they had probably set me up to assassinate Raphael.

Hypothesis: the Germans were behind the killings.

Somehow I wasn't convinced. The Germans, or their ODESSA agents, had tried to get rid of me three times already, and failed. Whoever the killer really was, I thought they were actually trying to help me.

It wasn't a comforting thought.

And then, how did Sophie fit into it? And how did Eldershott?

Fact: there was nothing in the briefing about *missing* angels, and I had to assume there weren't any.

Fact: I left behind me a room full of caged, broken angels. *Unknown* angels.

Question: where had they come from?

I remembered my dream again, the white, sterile land and, high above, angels flying on the winds.

Was that their real home? Had I somehow stumbled, in my dreams, on…on heaven?

Or had I been taken there for a reason?

And another question, working its way slowly into my mind like a thin drizzle of black water: Had the Nazis somehow found a way into it?

That would explain the captured angels.

But then, why hadn't the Archangels done anything about it?

There were too many questions, and the time to ask them was running out. I needed some answers. I needed to reach the core of this operation and break it apart. I took off the mufflers and left them behind me, and walked away to the sound of the diminishing screams, choosing paths almost at random, with a strange belief they would lead me to my destination.

I traversed the corridors of pale silent ice, meeting no-one. I was entering that same dream state as I had on the way here, and I tried to fight it, to wrest control of my mind from this alien intrusion. It was all about control, and always has been—but the influence over me was growing, leading me across a blank icy map as if it intimately knew the layout of this underground complex. It was a chessboard, and I was a pawn, and a hidden player was pushing me to the edge of that board towards checkmate.

It was about control, because that's what I have to have when the mission is in its final phase. I had to be in control of my actions, the organism shutting down all unimportant routines and concentrating on one thing: survival. I was losing that control and I knew I would have to break it if I wanted to survive.

The feeling had a more sinister quality to it than the one I'd had on the skis. I tried to turn back, to choose a different path, but my body disobeyed me as if the instructions from my brain were not reaching their destination, and I tried to fight that and the apathy that was stealing over me.

It wouldn't go away and then I punched the wall of ice on my left, hard, and again, and again, until blood came out and the pain exploded in bright shards of ice, cold, dead, distant stars shimmering before my eyes.

When I stopped, my hand was caked in blood and slivers of ice, and there was a small crater in the wall where it had cracked.

I tried to move in the opposite direction to the pull and succeeded, my movements my own again, and then I ran, ran in the opposite direction, and as I did I heard the great gushing sound of water behind me and knew they had flooded the corridor and that, unless I reached higher ground, and fast, I would very soon become a sculpture of cold, dead ice.

NINETEEN

"IT IS NICE of you to join us." He spoke German and, as he did, a horsewhip tapped against his leather boots, *tap*, *tap*, *tap*, in time to a rhythm only he could hear.

It was pointless to disseminate; there was no cover story here, no Anna Krojer or Marija Zita or Janet Gordon to hide behind, this was ground zero and there was nowhere else to go.

Nevertheless… "I'm sorry," I said, spreading my hands slowly, "I don't understand…?" I said it in English but it didn't seem to make much of an impression on him, and he smiled, showing teeth. There was a file by his side and I knew it was mine. They would have known who I was—or what I was, at the very least.

"I was under the impression you spoke German fluently," he said, still in the same language, still smiling. He had very bright, white teeth. He probably polished them every night as if they were gemstones.

Tap. Tap.

"Perhaps we can test it by cutting off one of your small fingers and see how you react?"

One of his bodyguards was standing on my right, a little back. I saw him reach for one of the surgical knives and knew they would happily do it, and that what I had do was to try and lengthen the time until they did decide to get rid of me, and try and make my move before then. It wasn't much of a plan but it was all I had.

"That," I said, carefully and in German, "won't be necessary." I let my hands drop to my sides and felt them relax, just a little, behind me.

He was immaculately dressed in a grey uniform without insignia. Riding boots, a horsewhip. Greying hair, a sensitive face grown podgy, eyes that could make the cold outside seem like a holiday in the sun, somewhere hot where they serve drinks with little umbrellas and play soothing music. His eyes said there would never be any more drinks with little umbrellas, that I would never see the sun. They were quite eloquent, for eyes.

The smile didn't leave his face. It was like a growth that couldn't be removed. He said, "Excellent. You are a remarkable woman, Shadow Executive Killarney. That is your codename, isn't it? Killarney? Our friends in the Fourth Directorate have quite a large file on you." He tapped the table. "As you can see."

"And you are?" I said, letting it ride.

I felt them shifting again behind me. Nervous bastards. There was one on either side of me, two more covering the door. And *Herr Doktor*, tap-tap-bloody-tap. They were all standard muscle boys, in fact, a little too standard: blond, blue-eyed, large, they all looked exactly like the pair I had killed on the train, as if Herr Doktor had found himself a way of manufacturing perfect Arians.

"Is the name really important?" he asked, still smiling. Still tapping. Tap. Tap.

Tap.

"The work will live on after the name is forgotten, after all."

"And your work involves torturing angels?" I had to keep him talking, keep thinking of a way out of this.

When the water came rushing into the corridor I was already running, the organism taking over completely, using up all available resources, have to get out of this, run faster, find a way up or a way out, and hurry up because the water is nearly there, touching you…

There had been a shuddering sound and a part of the floor dropped away behind me with a sickening thud. I stumbled but kept running as, behind me, more of the floor dropped away. Icicles flew in the air and one or two hit me, their edges as sharp as blades.

There was only one way to do it and I took it, putting the gloves back on and praying it would work, and then I jumped, a three-hundred-and-sixty degrees jump shortened to a hundred and eighty as the boots caught on the ceiling, spikes extending, and I broke the arc and swung the other way, catching the ceiling with my hands, the gloves extending and catching at the ice, the needles driving in hard, and I held on as, underneath me, the water rushed, too low to touch me.

There was a ventilation shaft only a short distance from me—if I could reach it. I wasn't convinced of the efficiency of the suit. I knew every second the contact with the ice could weaken and I could fall into the frozen waters below. I inched my way towards the ventilation shaft, clawing at the ice, and reached it just as the floor fell beneath me and I was left staring at a drop that was a guaranteed kill, hanging upside down from the ceiling of ice.

There was nothing else to do. I reached out, carefully, carefully, hooked the grill and pulled; it dropped away from the ceiling and crashed below. I thought I'd made it. I reached through the hole and found purchase and tried to pull myself up.

Then two sets of arms grabbed me and pulled me up, and I knew the game was up and that I was the piece most likely to be off the board next.

They lifted me up and I couldn't help but breathe in relief. It's not easy hanging upside-down on a wall of ice when the floor drops below you, and whatever the alternative, at that moment I was pleased to be back on something solid.

There were two of them in the small space, and they gave me a fright until I realised they were not the two I had killed on the train. One had a gun trained on me but fighting would have been useless anyway; they had me and I was too exhausted to fight, not right then at any point. I'd have to work out the best time for that later. If there was a later.

They led me away. It was some sort of space between spaces, but not a crawlspace as I'd thought. It was another corridor, with grills in the floor through which I glimpsed the ruined corridor below, and it ended with a door.

We stepped through it, passed through another set of corridors, and then we were in a plush office and the Nazi with the horsewhip was greeting me with that smile. I'd made a mental note to erase that smile sometime in the near future, using as violent a means as was available to me.

"What you must understand," he said, "is that we do not *torture* angels. We *study* them. And what fascinating creatures they are! Such interesting powers. We knew you were approaching long before you did, you see. They have such *use-ful* powers; if they can only be harnessed. I was quite amazed when you fought back against their influence—if you hadn't fought, you would have been standing here some time ago with none of the unpleasantness of the flood. Still—" he looked thoughtful for a moment "—it certainly provided me with some interesting data on you."

"Who *are* you?" I said again but, as I did, a suspicion was already forming in my mind; how many crazed Nazi doctors were this ruthless, and still at large? I thought of the cages of angels, the operating theatre, the precision, the fastidiousness. Who was there who could do those things?

He could read it in my face, and the smile never wavered; he nodded once as if confirming my thoughts.

I said, "Mengele."

He almost beamed. Instead, the smile remained, like a malignant tumour. All I needed to remove it was a knife. "Always a pleasure to be recognised."

He was known as the *Butcher of Auschwitz*; his medical experiments on prisoners in the death camp had been blood-ied, grotesque, inhuman; he had specialised in experiments on twins, on midgets, but he had picked anyone he liked from the long queues leading up to the gas chambers. He had selected them by pointing his whip, idly.

ODESSA had helped him disappear after the war; there were rumours, never proven, that he had lived in Argentina, though similar claims had been made for Egypt, Korea and one even placed him for a time in Borneo, where they'd cap-tured Eichmann in '59.

Apparently, however, they were all equally wrong.

"Where do they come from?" I said. "The angels."

He laughed, a short, unpleasant sound as cold as the walls and as ugly as his smile. "Isn't that the million-dollar question?" He looked pleased with himself for using the expression; it sounded odd in German. And, "You'll find out."

I let my muscles relax and got ready to make a move; I could take out the guy on my left and use his gun. It would be risky, but it might just work and what alternative did I have?

I was about to swing. Then, before I'd even begun to turn, something heavy connected with the back of my head without warning, and I fell into a darkness as solid and as hard as ice.

TWENTY

THERE WAS SOMETHING cold against my back and my head hurt; I tried to move, but my arms and feet were restrained and it was useless to fight. I opened my eyes to see a face above me like an ill, inconstant moon, watching me with calculated interest: Herr Doktor, putting on surgical gloves by the light of a lamp that was pointing directly at my face. His hands cast shadows over me. He flexed his fingers, cast fleeting dark spiders over me, and seemed satisfied.

Which wasn't exactly how I felt.

The light hurt, but the light also served to focus my mind and I remembered.

Falling into a darkness as solid and as hard as ice…

I'd awoken in a world ruled by darkness; shapes shifted in the absence of light, the sound of wings beating against impossible winds. The smell of sterility.

I could see despite the darkness, see in a strange inversion of light and dark in which the darkness was palpable and formed its own vision. There was no up or down, only the sound of the winds like a beating heart, and all around me silent, majestic angels flew, free and inhuman, through a world of nothingness.

Killarney. The voice reached through my ears and into my brain; the same voice I had heard before. In the world of ice which was, I was beginning to see, the same world, though perhaps viewed differently.

Killarney.

"What do you want?" I said. And, "This is only a dream."

In dreams you sometimes find truth.

"Are you incapable of talking straight? Because I am getting sick of the sphinx routine."

Careful, human, the voice said, and I felt myself lifted into the winds and held as they blew about me; angels swarmed and flew away from me.

I was held in a giant hand, obsidian-dark and craggy like a rock. "Point taken," I said, but my voice seemed to be carried away by the winds and disappeared before it reached my ears.

You have not long before you return to your world, the voice said. *When you wake up you will be in danger.*

"Really."

I felt giant fingers tighten on me; the sound of the winds was heightened.

You have only a short space of time left.

"Who are you?" It was a question I was rapidly getting used to asking.

When you wake up, the voice said, ignoring me, *you must locate the key. Locate and destroy it.*

"You mean Eldershott." It was a statement, not a question. I remembered my last dream—if it was a dream, which I was no longer sure of—and remembered the words. The giant had called Eldershott *the cipher and the key.* I wish I knew what in hell it was talking about.

I will be near you when the time comes. Be ready.

I felt myself lifted, higher and higher into the winds, and then the giant fingers opened and I was hurled down, down, down into a darkness as solid and as hard as ice…

"I see the patient is awake. Good." His voice was as emotionless as before, but the horsewhip was missing; I couldn't decide if that was a good or a bad thing.

His face loomed above mine. "You know, you are an incredibly resourceful woman. Really one of the most remarkable I have ever met. It will be an honour to study you."

"Where is Eldershott?" I had to keep him talking, anything to keep away the array of shining, utilitarian knives on the rack. Injecting a note of indignation into it: "What have you done with him?"

"Done? Done?" He beamed at me from above, a human angel of death. "We have done nothing to Dr Eldershott. I would thank you to remember his title. The man was undervalued by your people. *Vastly* undervalued. Dr Eldershott is a genius, and *I* certainly don't say that easily."

"Genius in what?" I demanded. "He's only a cryptographer, for God's sake! What did you need him for, a more secure code for your radios?"

It seemed to be working. Mengele seemed almost eager to talk, and I knew then that he wasn't planning to keep me alive.

"Only? Do you have any idea—" He broke off suddenly. "I can tell you really don't know. It would suggest that either your Control found it more useful not to brief you or, and this is remarkable, that your masters in London themselves have no idea of the work we do! How extraordinary!"

"What," I said calmly, "are you talking about?"

Instead of answering, Mengele turned and barked an order beyond my field of vision. Then he turned back to me. "Don't think that you can save yourself by drawing me to talk," he said. "All you would do is lengthen, however little, the wait for that which is inevitable." He sighed theatrically. "It would be a shame to kill you. As you can see, I am surrounded by very loyal servants, but servants are all they are."

"A big family of them."

"You noticed? I guess it *is* hard to miss." The eyes, searching my face. "The product of a breeding programme I have been running since the late thirties. Strong and, as I said, loyal. Unfortunately their intelligence isn't the highest—but where we are going they will have little need for that. Loyalty will suffice."

"Where you are going?" I said, and he was about to answer when I heard the shuffle of feet and Eldershott's worried, red face gazed down at me, his head floating like a disembodied balloon right next to Mengele's.

TWENTY-ONE

"WHAT IS SHE doing here?" His voice was petulant. He had dark rings round his eyes. "She took my book."

"But we got you another one," Mengele said soothingly. "As you can see—" this to me "—he feels very much at home here."

I couldn't see what he had based that observation on. Elder-shott looked at me for a while longer, a mixture of confusion and discomfort in his eyes. Then he'd seemingly had enough, and his head disappeared from my field of vision.

"What was so important about his book?" I said. "It was a textbook on military history of the world since the Coming. I had one at school."

Mengele's smile seemed to expand, the growth breathing on its own. "So appropriate, wouldn't you say?"

I needed time to think. Something big was going down, and I couldn't keep him talking forever. I needed a diversion, an opportunity to free myself before the crazy Nazi doctor took me apart for his amusement. Keep him talking, and pray.

I'd not prayed in years. I wondered if I still remembered how.

"As above, so below, Killarney," Mengele said, and I remembered the last time I had heard that expression, my first dream about the angels. "Tell her, *Dr* Eldershott. Tell her about your discovery."

Eldershott's face appeared again above mine. He blinked red eyes. "Why don't you just kill her?"

Mengele looked amused, then his expression changed. Hunger? Impatience? I couldn't quite tell. His head disappeared and I was left, for a moment, staring alone at Eldershott. He was my only chance.

"Sophie." I formed the word on my lips, whispered it at him like the whisper of an angel's wing. "Sophie wants you to help me."

He blinked at me rapidly. His expression changed from puzzled to eager to concerned, and he blinked again and tried to whisper something, and I shook my head, a tiny movement, and then Mengele's face returned to hover above mine. It looked worried. The smile pulsed on his face like a cancer at the approach of a surgeon's knife.

I threw a guess at him and said, "Are you expecting someone?"

"Enough." That smile was clinging on, but it was losing. I wondered what had cauterised it and hoped it had been me. He turned his head. "Please turn on the electricity, Dr Eldershott."

"The electricity, Dr Mengele? Are you sure?"

I did not like the direction their conversation was taking, did not like mention of electricity, did not like the look in Mengele's eyes when he looked at me. That smile of his wasn't gone, it was merely in remission.

"I'm not the only one who's been looking for you..." I said very softly, and his head whipped back and I could only pray, pray that me mentioning Sophie to Eldershott had worked, would work, that Eldershott might try and do something, perhaps sabotage the equipment.

But it wasn't necessary.

From somewhere far away I could hear a monstrous sound, like the cry of some vast shambling beast. It howled through the ice like a wind of frost, shaking the foundations.

Mengele shouted orders; soldiers ran, Eldershott blinked nervously, and I thought, *Miracles don't happen every day.*

I thought I was safe then.

I was wrong.

As the ground shuddered beneath, Mengele took one last look at me, put his smile back into place and pushed Eldershott aside. His hand reached beyond my field of vision. I heard the sound of a switch being pulled—

Then pain, more pain than I had ever felt before, tore through my skin and my brain and my nerves and I screamed until my screams drowned away that other sound, any other sound, until I was lost in an ocean of dark liquid pain and I drowned.

TWENTY-TWO

WHEN I OPENED my eyes, Eldershott's worried face hovered above mine. His hands fumbled at the restraints that held me bound.

"You have to be quick," he said. He said that listlessly. He looked like I felt.

After he'd freed me, I sat forward and wished I hadn't. My head throbbed with the sounds of a world war. My body felt as if it had been hit by a truck carrying nuclear waste.

"How do you feel?"

"I've been better."

It felt good not to be tied up. It felt good to not be dead.

There was still time for both those things to change.

When I glanced around the empty room, I saw there was a pool of vomit in the corner. Eldershott followed my glance and winced. "I do not approve of their methods," he said, primly. Now that I looked closely I could see traces of vomit caked at the corners of his mouth.

"Weak stomach?"

"I'm a scientist, not a…" He didn't seem to know how to finish that sentence.

I tried to smile at him. I should have been grateful. By being sick he had found the excuse to stay behind whilst I was being electrocuted to death and, like it or not, he had saved my life. I hoped it was worth saving.

I stood up. My legs supported me. Good legs. From somewhere far away a roar sounded.

"What's been happening?" I said—demanded. My legs still kept me upright. I took that as a good sign. The distant roar again, and the sound of gunshots, and I took a deep breath, trying to reach a far distant calm, all the while the organism feeling like a cat let out of a cage where it had been tortured, wanting to lash out and hurt, and kill.

Breathe, Killarney.

Breathe.

"You said Sophie wanted mfe to help you. So you should know. Some of it at least. Where is she?" He was like a child with his cryptic comments and sudden demands; I controlled the urge to smack him.

That sound again, in the distance. It seemed to climb through my feet and into my bones. "I can't wait. You'll have to stop it," he said. "I have to go before they become suspicious. I have to help them open the gate."

"Eldershott, wait—"

But with that he was gone, nervous gait leading him out of the torture chamber and away. The door closed softly behind him like an unanswered prayer.

Stop. Think. Breathe.

Execution time. I was entering the final phase of the operation and I knew it. Whatever plan the Nazis had, they were putting it into operation.

I had to stop them.

I was free and they didn't know it yet, and it would give me some room to manoeuvre. I had to follow Eldershott; somehow he was the key to all this but, at the same time, I had a score to settle, a very personal score with an elderly German scientist who should have been dead long ago.

I was going to help him on that road.

I tested my footing, performed a pirouette, didn't fall over. Decided it would have to do. I still had my suit on and that was good, but I needed weapons.

It turned out there were some in the other room.

I entered the lab area again; all around me broken angels cried through bars of ice. I didn't know what they could do; I didn't know if they were even capable of freedom, but they were my best chance and I took it. I went back to the operating room and grabbed some of Mengele's toys and brought them back with me.

A blowtorch. Good. The thought that he'd intended to use it on me just notched up another point on the score board. For now, I turned the blowtorch onto full power and began cutting the bars.

They steamed and broke, a strange material that was neither ice nor glass, and the angels stopped keening and stared at me with unreadable eyes through the broken bars of their cages.

"Come on!" I said. And "Shoo!" I waved my hands at them, feeling somewhat at a loss.

Slowly, they began to stagger out of the cages, and I could see for the first time how hurt they were. Scars covered their bodies, oozing puss that dried uneasily in a cornucopia of colours; some had only half a wing or none at all, and ugly wounds sprouted from their shoulder blades; others had eyes missing, or ears. They looked like naked pieces of flesh at a butcher's shop.

I hoped they'd live. I hoped they would provide the diversion I needed, if one was still needed. At least they would add to the general mayhem. I could hear guns being fired in the distance, and screams, some of them human.

I kept the torch and left the angels. As I stepped into the corridor beyond the torture chamber, two soldiers stumbled into my path; they didn't even acknowledge my presence but kept on running, looking back in fear.

I headed in that direction. The direction of the screams.

The screaming intensified the further I moved; at last I reached a wide, circular hall and stopped, holding onto the blowtorch like a promise. The scene in the hall permeated my senses slowly, and then its full meaning finally sank in.

TWENTY-THREE

THE THING THAT was Sophie Stockard stood in the centre of the room, perfectly motionless. She looked like a figurine carved out of driftwood, a still and fragile thing in the middle of chaos.

Filling my vision was the structure. Crude swastikas were carved into it, and angels' wings; it was a circle of strange metal, and I should have been able to see through it to the wall behind but I couldn't. Instead, the air inside the circle vibrated and hummed, acting at times like a mirror, at others, like opaque glass. Rows of machinery were lined up on each side of the structure; Sophie faced the humming circle, and opposite her was Mengele.

He was holding a gun to Eldershott's head.

As I approached them, Sophie's head swivelled towards me and that horrible voice said, *It is time.* It was the voice I had heard in Paris when Metatron had died, the same as I'd heard in Lubyanka; the same, I was beginning to realise, as I'd heard in my dreams; the voice of the giant in the land of the angels.

And out of the same mouth came Sophie Stockard's own voice, piercing through the noise—"Help him! He mustn't die!"

Whatever Sophie had been doing had momentarily stopped, it seemed. Fallen blocks of ice and broken, smoking machinery paid witness to the powers she had unleashed.

There were men in smocks working on the machines, and more of the identical blond soldiers watching them, guns at the ready. The air in the giant mirror hummed and twisted in impossible ways.

"One more move from you and he's dead," Mengele said. His voice carried in a suddenly silent hall.

He pushed Eldershott towards the bank of machines. The gun kept pointing at Eldershott's head. Mengele had surgeon's hands. They remained steady. "You have to finish what you've started, Dr Eldershott. Please, you must open the gateway." Behind him, soldiers began to stream into the room in silence, row upon row of blond, large men in uniforms on which the swastika and wings were clearly displayed.

Mengele's face twisted in sudden hatred. "How many years?" he shouted at the unmoving Sophie. "How many years since you brought your own petty war into ours? For years my people have worked to create a new, better world—before your creatures came. Your fallen angels. It is *you* who are responsible for the defeat we suffered, and it is *you* who will now pay the price.'

Sophie's face underwent a strange transformation as if two opposing forces were battling inside her, but neither of them seemed inclined to talk just then.

Mengele kept ranting. "You thought you could dump your losers on us, that you could carry on living in savagery with no care in the world. How long has it been since heaven was last challenged?"

He didn't look as if he expected an answer. People like him so seldom did. But he got one.

The war lasted many eons, the terrible voice said through Sophie's lips. *Those who challenged us were defeated. It seemed less cruel to send them to a physical prison than to have their essences snuffed out like candles made of human fat.*

"I could have taught you a thing or two about that," Mengele said.

I knew I had to do something quickly. I saw Eldershott begin to rock, Mengele's gun still trained on him. As he rocked harder, he began to sing. It was a high, reedy voice, the sound of a human sacrifice. The notes and the words made no sense, but I could feel their impact, see it in the gathering intensity of the shimmer that was the gate. I looked at Eldershott with new eyes. Thought back—

An academic, really, Turner had said, almost apologetically. *Cryptography, though you couldn't tell to look at him, good solid work but he wasn't that important.*

Cryptography. That, and an interest in angels. What code had he cracked? What door had he opened in the process?

The answer was before me now.

The gateway shimmered and changed. Beyond it, faintly, I could see pale blue skies, a whitewashed beach and in the distance, as small as birds, far-off angels in flight.

He had discovered the gateway to the world of the angels. Mengele had called it heaven, but I wondered if it really was. And if so, who was the giant who had visited me (or had I visited him?) in my dreams? The one who now seemed to possess Eldershott's girlfriend?

And what were the Nazis planning? An occupation of heaven?

I was about to charge him, terminate Eldershott as I was supposed to, try and end this.

But then the Archangel Raphael materialised in the centre of the hall and everything stopped.

TWENTY-FOUR

"*YOU*," THE THING that was Sophie Stockard said.

And, "Yes," said Raphael, his voice a frozen river.

By the gate, Eldershott has stopped moving. The image in the gateway began, slowly, to fade.

I should have killed you myself.

"If so, you should have done it a long time ago."

Yes...

Raphael turned his head and looked directly at me. His eyes were a bottomless grey, sucking me in. "You, I will kill slowly," he said. "Over more years than you can imagine."

I was fast becoming popular. First Mengele, now Raphael. It didn't help that I, too, had thought one of them was already dead.

You were planning a second revolt. Against me. You, whom I let live, you, whom I banished from my side, forever. You dare to threaten me?

"Hardly." Raphael almost smirked. "Only to retake what is rightfully ours."

You planned to invade our world with the aid of humans?

"Plan," Raphael said. "Not *planned*."

There was a moment of complete silence, as if sound, the *nature* of sound, were suddenly absent from the physical world.

Then Sophie's body began to convulse and the air about her grew hazy as if intense heat formed inside her mortal human shape.

Out of the haze, wings extended slowly, four, five, six metres in each direction; silver and sharp, they were like a bronze statue come to life in bass relief. The wings extended, then snapped.

And out of the circle of heat stepped God.

It is the only description I could think of. It was and wasn't the giant I had seen in that other world, and it was more than that: it was huge and all encompassing and kind and cruel and all things at once. It was an angel the like of which I had never seen before.

It didn't faze Raphael.

With a strangely human scream of rage, he attacked the bright angel. One wing extended and shot out, almost tearing through the other's bright façade. The thing that was once Sophie Stockard side-stepped him easily, and its own wing lashed and carved a deep wound in Raphael's torso.

It was hard to focus, but I had to. Glancing aside, I saw Mengele point the gun again at Eldershott, saw Eldershott begin to rock again, begin to mutter, begin to sing.

The heat from the Archangels' fight was melting a crater in the hall. I had to do something, had to stop Eldershott, banish the God-like being before it could kill again, before it started a third world war by its actions.

The cipher and the key. Destroy it. I remembered what it had said. I had to stop the Germans invading the angels' world; to fail would mean suicide for everyone on Earth. But I also had to stop the killings of the angels on Earth, or I would face the same outcome.

I formulated a plan but, before I could move, an awful, unearthly keening sound issued from behind me, and the first of the tortured angels I had freed stepped into the hall.

TWENTY-FIVE

WHEN THE ANGELS came through into the hall, madness took hold of them. They tried to fly and failed and that seemed to drive them even madder. They came crashing into the Nazi soldiers, ripping them with their wings, with their teeth, with their hands. Some attacked the gate, trying desperately to go through, crashing as they hit an invisible wall. The rest attacked Raphael, who drove them away easily as he battled his real opponent.

You dared to abduct my subjects? You dared to raid my world with what holes you had remaining through which to breach it? It was an awful voice, a voice like the heat of a nuclear reactor. They fought inside a rapidly-growing crater, and I looked at the ceiling, worried. Cracks were appearing in the ice, caused by the intense heat.

"As above, so below," Raphael cried, the tip of his wings nearly cutting his opponent in half. "And now our fellow humans will have all the angels they want for their experiments." A clash of wings as bright as the sun, and I was momentarily blinded. Then: "And when they're finished, I won't have even begun."

I had to reach Eldershott. The angels seemed to avoid me; for the two fighting in the ice I was forgotten, at least for the moment; and Mengele was too busy keeping his gun on Eldershott and the rest of his staff (who seemed to want nothing more than to disappear into thin air) to pay much attention to me.

I approached cautiously along the wall, trying to reach them. "Faster!" Mengele was shouting. "Faster!"

And Eldershott was praying, and the gateway was again filling up with images, bringing into existence a world beyond our world. I wasn't sure how many soldiers Mengele would have left when the broken angels were done with them, but I suspected there were more, somewhere, only now getting ready for their assault on heaven.

There was only one thing I could have done and so I did it; I approached the *back* of the gate. From that side it looked like a clear piece of glass through which I could see the rest of the hall. The structure itself looked solid, and I needed to unbalance it.

Then one of the angels flying at the screen cried, a single word, and disappeared inside the gate and I knew it was open, and that if it were to be closed it had to be now.

There were corpses belonging to the blond soldiers all round me. I went through their uniforms, picking up what I needed.

I returned to the base of the gate, and I was right: more soldiers were streaming in and the first few looked as though they were about to go through. I had to act fast.

Grenades. Take a bunch in one hand, pull the pin, dump, repeat on other side. Get the hell out of there. And counting. Counting all the time. Praying the numbers are right. Praying it would work. Praying it wouldn't kill me.

One. Two. Three.

Four.

Five!

Explosion.

Six.

Seven!

Explosion.

The gate shuddered—

Eight. Nine. Ten.

Eleven.

—and fell, slowly, forwards.

It was even larger than I'd thought. The Nazis seemed determined to go through it en masse.

And that was what I was counting on.

As it fell, it fell towards the centre, and I prayed it would hold, prayed Eldershott would keep up the contact for just a little while longer.

And it did. And he did.

The heavy structure of the gate came crashing down on Raphael and on the thing that was once Sophie Stockard and was now more, or less, God.

And when the circle passed over them, it swallowed them, and they disappeared.

Then, with a gun I had picked up from a dead soldier, I put a bullet through Eldershott's head.

TWENTY-SIX

I WAS RUNNING through the corridor pursued by confusion.

The ice was melting.

Behind me, swearing and screaming; German words mingling with angelic screeching.

They would die.

I ran until I reached the ladder I had first come through.

I climbed it.

Behind me, faint explosions. I had set the remainder of the grenades well.

I came out into glaring sunlight and the brightness of ice.

And ran.

No-one tried to stop me. No sniper-shot cut through my brain as through pliant water. I ran.

When I stopped and turned, I was far away and breathing hard. Behind me the research facility, that icy, enchanted castle, was beginning, slowly, to collapse.

Mengele would die in this way. A bullet would have been too merciful for him.

I watched the place fall down. Cracks in the ice, blocks falling down. Somewhere, the snow would be stained red.

The ice was settling. The earth shook. After a while, when I looked at it, all I could see was one more natural hill covered in snow.

It could almost have been peaceful.

The target had been reached and eliminated.

He was dead. Eldershott, Sophie…I couldn't save you. I am sorry. Men and women die when they involve themselves in the games of angels. It was a lesson learnt well.

There would be no war with the angels.

Not yet.

I turned and looked ahead. It would be a long walk to the pickup point.

The game we play is war, and it is cold, as cold as the ice around me as I walk. It is a strange world we live in, in which human and angel co-exist; there are more powers at play in the shadows than just us, the Bureau, the Fourth Directorate, Mossad… There are other shadows, other boards, other puppets and puppeteers. Others walk in the shadow world we tread.

I had averted a war. But for how long?

The sound of a solitary bird startled me, crying far away. Strange, that I had noticed no living creature here until now. Perhaps their instincts were better than mine.

Target reached and eliminated. Or something like that.

Every part of my body ached. For all that, the silence and the cold round me were comforting. The air had a fresh, clean smell mixed with earth, mixed with humanity and life. And the sun shone.

I was alive. I had come through.

I am alive.

Shadows lengthened. In the distance, I could see the plane waiting like a nesting bird on the ice.

I would go somewhere warm, I decided. Somewhere tropical, lush, sweaty. Somewhere far away from ice and angels.

I opened the door and climbed up into the seat, settling back with a sigh.

"Get us out of here," I said.

Without a word, Seago started the engines and then we were flying, flying high on the cold, clean winds.

Flying high as angels.

ABOUT THE AUTHOR

LAVIE TIDHAR IS author of *Osama*, *The Violent Century*, *A Man Lies Dreaming*, *Central Station*, and *Unholy Land*, as well as the Bookman Histories trilogy. His latest novels are *By Force Alone*, children's book *The Candy Mafia* and comics mini-series *Adler*. His awards include the World Fantasy Award, the British Fantasy Award, the John W. Campbell Award, the Neukom Prize and the Jerwood Fiction Uncovered Prize.

FOR NEWS ABOUT JABBERWOCKY BOOKS AND AUTHORS

Sign up for our newsletter*: http://eepurl.com/b84tDz
visit our website: awfulagent.com/ebooks
or follow us on twitter: @awfulagent

THANKS FOR READING!

*We will never sell or give away your email address, nor use
it for nefarious purposes. Newsletter sent out quarterly.